DANGER MOON

By
FREDERIK POHL

I0616777

ARMCHAIR FICTION
PO Box 4369, Medford, Oregon 97504

For more information about Armchair Books and products, visit our website at…

www.armchairfiction.com

Or email us at…

armchairfiction@yahoo.com

ON THE MOON, THERE'S MORE THAN MEETS THE EYE...

Steve Templin had worked as a professional trouble-shooter for years, but now he wanted something different in his life. It wasn't going to be easy, though, and it certainly wasn't going to be cheap. And when Ellen Bishop, owner of Terralune Projects, asked for his help, he agreed... for a price. Something strange was happening to her father's Lunar mining firm and she needed someone like Templin to get to the bottom of it. As he weighed into the situation, he discovered a web of sabotage, greed, and murder—and soon after, the remains of an ancient alien race.

Here is another engaging and highly entertaining tale from a master of science fiction, the late, great Frederik Pohl.

FOR A SECOND COMPLETE NOVEL, TURN TO PAGE 95

CAST OF CHARACTERS

STEVE TEMPLIN
Reporting for a mysterious mission on the Moon, he had to do more than find saboteurs—he had to expose their deadly motive.

ELLEN BISHOP
Her father had died, leaving her with a vast Lunar mining company—along with all of the dangers facing it.

JOE OLCOTT
A very rich, very greedy man who had a plan to become owner of all mining operations on the moon!

JIM CULVER
Assigned as Templin's assistant, he tried to help sort out the finer points of what appeared to be a massive sabotage plot.

THE LUNARIANS
They were the original inhabitants of the Moon, with a very strong dislike for anything human.

SAM BLIGH
He was the power engineer for Terralune and he needed to keep the plant running—even in the face of sabotage.

CHAPTER ONE

STEVE TEMPLIN came out of the airlock into Hadley Dome and looked around for someone to blow off steam on. Templin was fighting mad—had been that way for three days now, ever since he was ordered to report for this mysterious mission on the Moon.

Templin stripped off his pressure suit and almost threw it at the attendant. "I'm looking for Ellen Bishop," he growled. "Where can I find her?"

The attendant said deferentially, "Miss Bishop's suite is on Level Nine, sir. Just below the solarium."

"Okay," groused Templin, walking off.

"Just a second, sir," the attendant called after him. "You forgot your check. And who shall I say is calling, please?"

Templin took the metal tag and jammed it in the pocket of his tunic. "Say nothing," he advised over his shoulder. "I'm going to surprise her."

He stared contemptuously around the ornate lobby of Hadley Dome, then, ignoring the waiting elevator, headed for the wide basalt stairway that led upstairs. With the force of gravity here on the Moon only about one sixth as powerful as on the surface of the Earth, an elevator was a particularly useless and irritating luxury. It was fit, Templin thought, only for the kind of washed-out aristocrats who could afford to chase thrills for the five hundred dollars a day it cost them to live in Hadley Dome. Templin, a heavyweight on his home planet, weighed little over thirty-

five pounds on the Moon. He bounded up the stairs in great soaring leaps, eight or ten steps at a time.

On the ninth level he paused, not even winded, and scowled about him. All over were the costly trappings of vast wealth. To Templin's space-hardened mind, Hadley Dome was a festering sore spot on the face of the Moon. He glowered at the deep-piled Oriental carpet on the floor, the lavish murals that had been painted on the spot by the world's highest priced artists.

Someone was coming down the long hall. Templin turned and saw a dark, solidly built man coming toward him in the peculiar slow-motion walk that went with the Moon's light gravity. Templin stopped him with a gesture.

"I'm looking for Ellen Bishop," Templin repeated wearily. "Where's her room?"

THE DARK man stopped and looked Templin over in leisurely fashion. Judging by the gem-studded belt buckler that adorned his brilliantly colored shorts, he was one of the Dome's paying guests...which meant that he was a millionaire at the least. He said in a cold, confident voice, "Who the devil are you?"

Templin clamped his jaw down on his temper. Carefully he said, "My name is Templin. Steve Templin. If you know where Ellen Bishop's room is, tell me; otherwise skip it."

The dark man said thoughtfully, "Templin. I know that name—oh, yes. You're that crazy explorer, aren't you? The one who's always hopping off to Mercury or Venus or some other planet."

"That's right," said Templin. "Now look, for the last time—"

"What do you want to see Ellen Bishop about?" the dark man interrupted him.

Templin lost control. "Forget it," he flared. He started to walk past the dark man, but the man held out his arm and stopped him. Templin halted, standing perfectly still. "Look, mister," he said. "I've had a tough day, and you're making me mad. Take your hand off my arm."

The dark man said angrily, "By heaven, I'll have you thrown out of the Dome if you don't watch your tongue! I'm Joe Olcott!"

Templin deliberately shook the man's arm off. The dark man growled inarticulately and lunged for him.

Templin sidestepped easily. "I warned you," he said, and he brought his fist up just hard enough to make a good solid contact with the point of Olcott's jaw. Olcott grunted and, grotesquely slowly in the light gravity, he collapsed unconscious on the carpeted floor.

A gasp from behind told Templin he had an audience. He whirled; a girl in the green uniform of a maid was frozen in the doorway of one of the rooms, one hand to her mouth in an attitude of shock.

Templin saw her and relaxed, grinning. "Don't get upset about it," he told her. "He was asking for it. Now maybe *you* can tell me where Ellen Bishop's room is?"

The maid stammered, "Y—yes, sir. The corner suite, at the end of the corridor."

"Thanks."

The maid hesitated. "Did you know that that was Mr. Joseph Olcott?" she asked tentatively.

Templin nodded cheerfully. "So he told me." In a much-improved frame of mind he strolled down to the door the maid had indicated. He glanced at it disapprovingly—it was carved of a single massive piece of oak, which was rare treasure on the treeless, airless moon—but shrugged and rapped it with his knuckles.

"Come in," said a girl's voice from a concealed loudspeaker beside the door, and the door itself swung open automatically. Steve walked in and discovered that he was in a well-furnished drawing room, the equal of anything on Earth.

From behind a huge desk a girl faced him. She was about twenty, hair black as the lunar night, blue eyes that would have been lovely if they had any warmth.

Templin looked around him comfortably, then took out a cigarette and put it in his lips. The chemically treated tip of it kindled to a glow as he drew in the first long puff. "I'm Steve Templin," he said. "What do you want to see me about?"

A TRACE of a smile curved the corners of the girl's red mouth. "Sit down, Mr. Templin," she said. "I'm glad you're here."

Templin nodded and picked out the chair closest to the desk. "I'm not," he said.

"That's hardly flattering."

Steve Templin shrugged. "It isn't intended to be. I went to work for your father because I liked him and because he gave me a free hand. After he died and you took over, I renewed my contract with the company because it was the only way I saw to keep on with my work on the Inner Planets. Now—I don't know. What do you want with me here?"

Ellen Bishop sighed. "I don't know," she confessed. "Maybe if I knew, I wouldn't have had to cancel your orders to go back to Mercury. All I know is that we need help here, and it looks like you're the only one who can provide it."

Steve asked non-committally, "What kind of help?"

The girl hesitated. "How long have you been out of touch with what's going on?" she countered.

"You mean while I was on Mercury? About eleven months; I just got back."

Ellen nodded. "And has anyone told you about our—trouble here?"

Steve laughed. "Nobody told me anything," he said flatly. "They didn't have time, maybe. I came back from Mercury with survey charts that took me six months to make, showing where there are mineral deposits that will make anything here on the Moon look sick. All I wanted to do was turn them over to the company, pick up supplies, and start out for Venus. And one of your glorified office boys was waiting for me at Denver skyport with your ethergram, ordering me to report here. I just about had time for one real Earth meal and a bath before I caught the rocket shuttle to the moon."

"Well—" the girl said doubtfully. "Suppose I begin at the beginning, then. You know that my father organized this company, Terralune Projects, to develop uranium deposits here on the Moon. He raised a lot of money, set up the corporation, and made plans. He even arranged to finance trips to other planets, like yours to Mercury and Venus, because doing things like that meant more to him than making money. And then he died."

Her face shadowed. "He died," she repeated, "and I inherited a controlling interest in Terralune. And then everything went to pot."

A buzzer sounded on Ellen Bishop's desk, interrupting her. She said, "Hello," and a voice-operated switch turned on her communicator.

A man's voice drawled, "Culver speaking. Shall I come up now?"

Ellen hesitated. Then she said, "Yes," and flicked off the communicator. "That's Jim Culver," she explained. "He'll be your assistant while you're here."

"That's nice," Templin said acidly. "Assistant to do what?"

The girl looked surprised. "Oh I didn't tell you, did I? You're going to manage the uranium mines at Hyginus Cleft."

TEMPLIN OPENED his eyes wide and stared at her. "Look, Bishop," he said, "I can't do that. What do I know about uranium mines—or any other kind of mines?"

Before the girl could answer, the door opened. A tall, lean man drifted in, looked at Templin with mournful eyes. "Hello," he said.

Templin nodded at him. "Get back to the question," he reminded the girl. "What about these mines? I'm no miner."

The girl said, "I know you aren't. We've had three mining engineers on the project in eight weeks. Things are no better for them—in fact, things are worse; ask Culver." She waved to the lean man, who was fumbling around his pockets for a cigarette.

Culver found the cigarette and nodded confirmation. "Trouble isn't ordinary," he said briefly. "It's things that are—strange. Like machines breaking down. And tunnels caving in. And pieces of equipment being missing. Nothing that a mining engineer can handle."

"But maybe something that *you* can handle." Ellen Bishop was looking at Templin with real pleading in her eyes, the man from the Inner Planets thought. He said, "Got any ideas on who's causing it? Do you think it's just accidental? Or have you been having trouble with some other outfit, or anything of the sort?"

Ellen Bishop bit her lip. "Not real trouble," she said. "Of course, there's Joe Olcott…"

Joe Olcott. The name rang a fire-bell in Templin's mind. Olcott…yes, of course! The chunky dark man in the corridor—the one he had knocked out!

He grinned abruptly. "I met Mr. Olcott," he acknowledged. "Unpleasant character. But he didn't seem like much of a menace to me."

Ellen Bishop shrugged. "Perhaps he isn't. Oh, you hear stories about him, if you can believe them. They say he has been mixed up in a number of things that were on the other side of the law—that he has committed all sorts of crimes himself. But—I don't really believe that. Only, it seems funny that we had no trouble at all until Olcott tried to buy a controlling interest in Terralune. We turned him down—it was just a month or so after Dad died—and from then on things have gone from bad to worse."

Templin stubbed out his cigarette, thinking. Automatically his fingers went to his pocket, took out another, and he blew out a huge cloud of fresh smoke. Then he stood up.

"I think I get the story now," he said. "The missing pieces I can fill in later. You want me to take charge of the Terralune mines here on the Moon and try to get rid of this jinx, whatever it is. Well, maybe I can do it. The only question is, what do I get out of it?"

Ellen Bishop looked startled. "Get out of it? What do you mean?" she demanded. Then a scornful look came into her ice-blue eyes. "Oh, I see," she said. "Naturally, you feel that you've got us at your mercy. Well—"

Templin interrupted her. "I asked you a question," he reminded. "What do I get out of it?"

She was seething under the surface. "Name your price," she said bitterly.

"Uh-uh." Templin shook his head. "I don't want money; I want something else."

"Something else?" she repeated in puzzlement. "What?"

Templin leaned across the desk. "I want to go back," he said. "I want a whole fleet of rocket ships to go back to Venus with me...lots of them, enough to start a colony. There's uranium on the Moon, and there are precious metals on Mercury...but on Venus there's something that's more important. There's a raw planet there, a whole world just like the Earth with trees, and jungles, and animals. And there isn't a human being on it. I want to colonize it—and I want Terralune Projects to pay the bill."

Ellen Bishop stared at him unbelievingly, and a slow smile crept into her lips. She said, "I beg your pardon...Temp. All right. It's a bargain." She grasped his hand impulsively. "If you can make the uranium mines pay-out I'll see that you get your ships. And your colony. And I'll see that you can take anyone you like on the Terralune payroll along with you to get started."

"Sold," said Templin. He released her hand, wandered thoughtfully over to the huge picture window that formed one entire wall of the girl's room.

AT A TOUCH of his fingers the opaque covering on the window opened up like a huge iris shutter, and he was gazing out on the barren landscape of the Moon. The Dome was on the peak of Mt. Hadley, looking out on a desolate expanse of twisted, but comparatively flat, rock, bathed in a sultry dull red glow of reflected light from the Earth overhead. Beyond the plain was an awesome range of mountains, the needle sharp peaks of them picked out in brilliant sunlight as the Sun advanced slowly on them.

Culver said from behind him, "That's what they call the Sea of Serenity."

Templin chuckled. *"Mare Serenitatis,"* he said. "I know. I've been here before—fourteen years ago, or so."

Ellen bishop amplified. "Didn't you know, Culver? Temp was one of Dad's crew when the old *Astra* landed here in 1957. I don't remember the exact order any more—were you the third man to step on the surface of the Moon, or the fourth?"

Templin grinned. "Third. Your father was fourth. First he sent the two United Nations delegates off to make it all nice and legal; then, being skipper of the ship, he was getting set to touch ground himself. Well, it was his privilege. But he saw me hanging around the air lock—I was a green kid then—and he laughed and said, 'Go ahead, Temp,' and I didn't stop to argue." Templin sobered, and glanced at Ellen Bishop. "I've had other jobs offered me," he said, "and some of them sounded pretty good, but I turned them down. Maybe it isn't smart to tell you this, but there's nothing in the world that could make me quit the company your father founded. Even though he's dead and a debutante is running it now."

He grinned again at her, and moved toward the door. "Coming, Culver?" he asked abruptly. The tall man nodded and followed him. "So long," said Templin at the door, and closed it behind him without waiting for an answer.

CHAPTER TWO

THEY PUT on their pressure suits and stepped out of the lock onto the hard rock outside. Culver gestured and led the way to a small crater-hopping rocket parked a few hundred yards from the Dome. It was still eight days till sunrise, and overhead hung the wide, solemn disk of the Earth, bright enough to read by, big as a huge, drifting balloon.

Mount Hadley is thrust into the dry Sea of Serenity like an arrowhead piercing a heart. Like all the Moon's surface it is bare rock, and the tumbled mountain ranges that lie behind it are like nothing on the face of the Earth. Templin stared around curiously, remembering how it had seemed when that first adventuring flight had landed there. Then he loped over the pitted rock after Culver's swollen pressure suit.

Culver touched a key ring inset in the rocket's airlock, and the door swung open. They scrambled aboard, closed the outer door, and Culver touched a valve that flooded the lock with air. Then they opened the inner door and took off their pressure suits.

Culver said, "The Terralune mine is up at Hyginus Cleft, about four hundred miles south of here. We'll make it in twenty minutes or so."

Templin sat down in one of the bucket seats before the dual controls. Culver followed more slowly, strapping himself in before he reached for the jet control levers. His ship was a little two-ton affair, especially designed for use on the surface of the Moon; powered with chemical fuel, instead of the giant atomics on larger ships, it could carry two persons and a few hundred pounds of cargo—and that was all.

He fed fuel to the tiny jets, paused to give the evaporators a chance to warm up, then tripped the spark contact. There was a brief sputter and a roar. As he advanced the jet lever a muffled grating sound came from underneath, and there was a peculiar jolting, swaying sensation as the rocket danced around on its tail jets for a moment before taking off.

And then they were jet-borne.

Culver swept up to a thousand feet and leveled off, heading toward a huge crater on the horizon. "My first landmark," he explained to Templin.

Templin nodded silently, staring out at the horizon. Although the sun itself was not yet visible, from their elevation it was just below the horizon curve. As they swept over a depression in the Moon's wrinkled surface Templin caught a glimpse of unendurable brightness where the sun was—a long, creeping tongue of flame that writhed in a slow snake curl. It was the sun's corona—a rare sight on the Earth, but always visible on the Moon, where there was no atmosphere to play tricks and blot it out.

Culver said curiously, "I didn't know you were one of the early Moon explorers. How come you aren't a millionaire, like the rest of them?"

Templin shrugged. "I keep on the move," he said ambiguously. "Yes, there were plenty of deals, I could have claimed mining rights, or signed up for lecture tours, or let some rocket-transport company pay me a fat salary for the privilege of putting my name on their board of directors. But I didn't want it. This way, Terralune pays me pretty well for scouting around the Inner Planets for them. I just put the checks in the bank, anyhow—where I spend my time, you can't spend your money. Money doesn't mean anything on Venus."

Culver nodded. His fingers danced skillfully over the jet keys as the nose of the rocket wavered a hairbreadth off course. Under control, the ship came around a couple of degrees until it was again arrowing straight for its target on the horizon, hurtling over the ancient, jagged face of the Moon.

Culver said casually, "I sort of envy you, Temp. It must be a terrific feeling to see things that no man has ever seen before. I guess that's why I came to the Moon, looking for things like that. But heaven knows, it's getting more like Earth—and the slums of the Earth, at that—every day. Ever since they put that Dome on Mount Hadley the place has been crummy with billionaire tourists."

Templin nodded absently. His attention was fixed on the rearview periscope. He frowned. "Culver," he said. "What's that coming up behind us?"

CULVER glanced at the scope. "Oh, that. Pleasure rocket. Looks like Joe Olcott's ship—he's got about the biggest space-yacht around. Only his isn't really a pleasure ship, because he pulled some political strings and got himself a vice-commander's commission in the Security Patrol, which means that his yacht rates as an auxiliary. No guns on it, of course; but the Patrol pays his fuel bills."

"A sweet racket," said Templin. "But what the devil is he so close for? If he doesn't watch out he's going to get his nose blistered. Way he's going now he'll be blasting right into our rocket exhaust."

Culver stared worriedly at the periscope. The fat bullet-shaped rocket yacht behind them was getting bigger in the scope, little more than a mile behind them. Then he exhaled. "There he goes," said Culver. The other ship swung its nose a few degrees off to the west. It was a big fast job, burning twice as much fuel as their light crater-jumper, and it slid past them not more that a quarter of a mile away, going in the same direction.

"Joe Olcott," said Templin. "I begin to think that I'm not going to like Mr. Olcott. And I'm pretty sure he doesn't like me; his jaw will be sore for a day or two to help him remember."

Culver grinned and fumbled in his pockets for a cigarette. "He's one of the billionaire tourists I was telling you about, Temp," he said. He sucked on the cigarette, puffed out blue smoke which the air purifiers drew in. "Olcott's about the worst of the bunch, I guess. Not only is he a rich man, but he's mixed up in—Hey! What're you doing?"

Culver squawked in surprise as Templin, swearing incandescently, dove past him to get at the jet controls. Then Culver's eyes caught what Templin had seen a fraction of a second earlier. The big, bullet-shaped rocket had passed them, then come around in a wide are, plunging head-on at their little ship at a good fifty-mile-a-minute clip.

Templin, sputtering oaths, was clawing at the controls. Under his frantic fingers their ship came slowly over...too slowly. The bullet-shaped ship, carrying twice their jets, came at them until it was a scant hundreds of yards away. Then it switched ends in a tight 10-gravity power turn. When the steering jets had brought it around the space yacht's pilot fed full power to his main-drive jets.

And deadly, white-hot gases from the rocket exhausts came flaring at Templin and Culver.

THE LITTLE ship quivered in a death-agony. Templin, white-lipped and soundless now, did the only thing left to him. He cut every jet; the crater-jumper was tossed about in the torrent of flaming gasses from the other ship and hurled aside. The Moon's gravity drew it down and out of danger. Then Templin thrust over the main-drive jets again, checking their fall in a fierce deceleration maneuver. The impact almost blanked Culver out; for a moment dark red specks floated before his eyes. When his vision cleared, he found them settling on their jets in the middle of a five-acre rock plain that formed the center of a small crater.

Templin fought the controls until the landing-struts touched rock. Then he cut jets; the swaying, unstable motion ceased and they were grounded.

Culver shook his head dazedly. "What the devil happened?" he gasped.

"Wait!" Templin's voice was urgent. Culver looked at him in astonishment, but held his tongue. Templin sat stock-still for a second, his bearing one of extreme concentration. Then he relaxed. "Don't hear any escaping air," he reported; "I guess the hull's still in one piece." He peered through the vision port at the black star-filled sky overhead. The long trail of rocket flame from the other ship came around in a sweeping curve that circled over them twice. Then, apparently satisfied, the other pilot straightened out. The flame trail pointed straight back the way they had come as the space yacht picked up speed. In a moment it was out of sight.

Templin smiled a chill smile. "He thinks he got us," he said. "Let him go on thinking so—for now."

"Tell me what that was all about." Culver demanded. "Two years I've been on the Moon, and nothing like this has ever happened to me before. What in heaven's name was he trying to do?"

Templin looked at him mildly. "Kill us, I should think," he said. "He came close enough to it, too."

"But why?"

Templin shrugged. "That's what I mean to find out. It might be because he's the man I slugged back in the Dome—but I doubt it. Or it might be because he thinks I can put Terralune's mine back on its feet. Wish I shared his confidence."

He unbuckled his safety straps and stood up. "This tub got a radio?" he demanded.

Culver, still pondering over what he had said, looked at him glassily a second. "Radio? Oh-no, of course not. Ship radios don't work on the Moon. You should know that."

Templin grinned. "When I was here there weren't any other ships to radio to. *Why* don't ship radios work?"

"Not enough power. It's not like the Earth, you know—any little one-watt affair can broadcast there, because the signals bounce off the Heaviside Layer. But you can't radio to anything on the Moon unless you can see it, because there isn't any Heaviside Layer to reflect radio waves, and so they only go in straight lines."

"How about the radio at the Dome?"

Culver shrugged. "That's a big one; that one bounces off the Earth's Heaviside Layer. What do you want a radio for, anyhow?"

"Wanted to save time," Templin said succinctly. "No matter. Come on, we've got a job of inspection to do. Put on your pressure suit."

Culver began complying automatically. "What are we going to do?"

"Make an external inspection. The way we were being kicked around up there, I want to make sure our outside hull is okay before I take this thing up again. Let's go look."

THE TWO men slipped into airtight pressure suits, sealed the helmets and stepped lightly out onto the lunar surface.

Templin skirted the base of the rocket, carefully examining every visible line and marking on the metal skin with the help of a hand-light. Then he said into his helmet radio, "Looks all right, Culver. By the way, what's that thing over there?"

He pointed to something that gleamed, ruddily metallic, at the base of the crater wall. Culver followed the direction of his arm.

"That's a rocket-launching site," he said. "Good place to stay away from. It's a hangover from the Three Day War—you know, when the boys got the idea they could conquer Earth by blasting it with atom-rockets from the Moon."

Templin nodded. "I remember," he said grimly. "My home town was one of the first cities wiped out. But why is it a good place to avoid?"

Culver scowled. "Wild radiations. They had a plutonium pile to generate power, and in the fighting the thing got out of control and blew its top. Scattered radioactive matter for half a mile around. Most of it's dead now, of course—these isotopes have pretty short half-lives. But the pile's still there."

Templin said, "And there it can stay, for all of me. Well, let's get moving. The ship looks intact to me—if it isn't, we'll find out when we put the power on."

Culver followed him into the ship's tiny pressure chamber. When they were able to take their helmets off he said curiously, "What's your next move, Temp? Going to get after Olcott?"

"That I don't know yet. One thing is for sure—that was no accident that just happened; he really wanted to blast us. And he had the stuff to do it with, too, with that baby battleship he was flying. It wasn't his fault that we ducked and only got a little dose of the tail end of his rocket blast... Get in the driver's seat, Culver. The sooner we get to the mine, the sooner the next round starts!"

THREE HOURS later, Templin was down in the mine galleries at Hyginus Cleft, staring disgruntedly at the wreck of a Mark VII digging machine. This was Gallery Eight richest vein of uranium ore they had found; just when the Mark VII had really begun to turn out sizeable amounts of metal there had been a shift in the rock underneath, crumbling the supports and bringing the shaft's ceiling down to pin the machine. Now the Mark VII, looking like a giant, steel-clad bug on its glittering caterpillar treads, was just half a million dollar's worth of junk.

Culver told him, "Tim Anson here was running the machine when the cave-in started; he can tell you all about it."

Templin looked at the man Culver had indicated—a short space-suited figure whose face was hidden behind an opaque mask. The mines were worked in vacuum, of course; it would have been impossible to keep the shafts filled with air. And the dangerous radiations present in the uranium ore required a special helmet for all who stayed long within range of them—a plastic material that transmitted light and other harmless rays in only one direction; dangerous rays it did not transmit at all. Templin said, "What about it, Anson? What happened?"

The man's voice came into his helmet radio. "There's nothing much to tell, sir," it said. "We opened this shaft 'bout a week ago and got some very pretty samples out of it. So we put the Mark Seven in, and I was on it when all of a sudden it began to shake. I thought the machine had gone haywire somehow, so I shut it off. But the shaking kept up, so I hopped off and beat it toward the escape corridor. And then the roof came down. Good thing I was off it, too; smashed the drivers seat like a tin toy."

Templin scowled. "Don't you survey these galleries?" he demanded of Culver. "If there was a rock fault underneath, why didn't you find out about it before you brought the Mark Seven down?"

Culver spread his hands. "Believe it or not, Temp, we surveyed. There wasn't any fault."

Templin glared at him. Before he could speak, though, a new voice said tentatively, "Mr. Templin? Message from the radio room." It was another miner holding a sheet of thin paper in his gauntleted hand. Templin took the flimsy from him and held it up to his faceplate. In the light of the helmet lamp he read:

Pilot Rocket Silvanus registry Joseph Olcott reported accident as required by Regulations. Report stated your Rocket not seen until collision almost inevitable then evasive action taken but impossible to avoid rocket exhaust striking your ship. Pilot reprimanded and cautioned. Signed: Stephens, HQ Lunadmin Tycho Crater.

Templin grinned leanly and passed the radio from Lunar Administration over to Jim Culver. "I squawked to Tycho about our little brush with Olcott," he explained.

Culver read it quickly and his face darkened with anger. Templin said over the inter-suit radio, "Don't get excited, Culver—I didn't expect anything better. After all, it stood to reason that Olcott would report it as an accident. He had to, in case we survived. At least, now we know where we stand." He glanced around the mine gallery, then frowned again. "I've seen enough," he said abruptly. "Let's go upstairs again."

Culver nodded and they walked back to the waiting monorail ore car. They stepped in, pressed the release button and the tiny wheels spun round. The car picked up speed rapidly; half a minute later it slowed and stopped at the entrance to the shaft. They crossed an open space, then walked into the air lock of the pressurized structure where Terralune's miners lived.

IN THE office Templin stripped off his pressure suit and immediately grabbed for one of his cigarettes. Culver more slowly followed his example, then sat down facing Templin. "You've seen the picture now, Temp," he said. "Do you have any ideas on what we can do?"

Templin grimaced. "In a negative sort of way."

"What do you mean?"

"Well, up to a little while ago I had a pretty definite idea that it was Joe Olcott who was causing all our trouble. That, I figured, I could handle—in fact, you might say I was sort of looking forward to it. But, although Olcott is a rich and powerful man and all that, I don't see how he can cause earthquakes."

Culver nodded. "That's it," he said soberly. "That's not the first time it's happened, either. We've had other kinds of trouble—broken machinery, mistakes in judgement, that sort of thing. Like you, I thought Olcott might be behind it. But—well, good Lord, Temp. The Moon is an old, old planet. There isn't even any internal heat anymore—it's all cooled off, and you'd think that its crust would have finally settled by this time. And yet...earthquakes keep on happening. Five of them so far."

Templin grunted and chucked away his cigarette. "Get the straw-bosses in here," he said. "Let's have ourselves a conference; maybe somebody will come up with an idea."

Culver flicked on a communicator and spoke into it briefly. He made four or five calls to different stations on the intercom set, then turned it off. "They'll all be here in about five minutes," he reported.

"Okay," said Templin. He pointed to a map on the wall behind Culver. "What's that?" he asked.

Culver turned. "That's the mine and environs, Temp. Right here—" he placed his finger on the map—"is the living quarters and administration building, where we are. Here's the entrance to the shafts. Power plant—that's where the solar collectors are. You know we pick up sunlight on parabolic mirrors, focus it on a heat exchanger and use it to generate electricity. This over here is the oxygen plant."

"You mean, we make our own oxygen?"

"Well, sort of. There's a lot of quartz on the Moon's surface, and that's silicon dioxide, as you ought to know. We electrolyze it and snatch out the oxygen."

Templin nodded. "What about this marking up on top of the map?"

Culver grinned. "That's our pride and joy here, Temp. It's an old Loonie city. Heaven knows how old—it's all run down into the ground now. Must be a million years old, maybe, but nobody knows for sure. But the Lunarians, whoever they were, really built for keeps—some of the buildings are still standing. Want to go over and take a look at it later?"

Templin hesitated. "No, not today," he said regretfully. "That's pleasure, and pleasure comes later."

There was a knock on the door. Culver yelled, "Come in," and it opened. A middle-aged, worried-looking man came in.

Culver introduced him. "Sam Bligh," he said. "Sam's our power engineer."

Templin shook hands with Bligh, then with half a dozen other men who followed him through the door. When all were gathered he stood up and spoke to them.

"My name's Templin," he said. "I'm going to be running this project for a while. I didn't ask for the job, and I don't want it, but I seem to be stuck with it. The sooner we begin producing, the sooner you'll get rid of me." He looked around. "Now, one at a time," he said. "I want to hear your troubles…"

The conference lasted about an hour. Then Templin said his piece. "There's going to be some ore brought out in the next twenty-four hours," he said. "I don't care what we have to do to do it, but we are going to ship at least one shipload of the stuff this week. And two shiploads next week, and three the week after, until we're up to quota. That clear?" He looked around the room. The men in it nodded. "Okay," he said. "Let's get going."

CHAPTER THREE

TWENTY-FOUR hours later, according to the big Terrestrial clock that hung in the ebony sky, Templin stood space-suited at the portal of the mine and watched the first monocar-load of uranium ore come out. On the ground at his feet was a flat black box, the size of an overnight bag. When the hoist crews had unloaded the glittering fragments of ore and stowed them in the hold of a freight rocket, Templin said over the radio, "Hold it up. Culver; don't send the monorail back down. I want to take another look at Gallery Eight."

Culver, supervising the unloading, said, "Sure, Temp; I'll tag along with you." He sprang lightly into the monorail. Templin, picking up the black box, followed and they braced themselves for the acceleration.

As the car picked up speed, they hurtled down the winding mine tunnels, lighted only by the headlights of the car itself. Though there was no air to carry sound, they could feel the vibration of the giant wheels on the single metal track as a deep, shuddering roar. Then the roar changed pitch as the car's brakes were set by the braking switch at the end of the line. The car slowed and stopped.

They got off and stepped down the rough-hewn gallery to where eight workmen were half-heartedly trying to clear the rock from the pinned Mark VII digging machine.

They stopped work to look at Templin. Templin said, "Go ahead, boys; we're just looking around." He moved toward the Mark VII, Culver following, studying the cave-in. Gallery Eight was seven hundred feet below the surface of the Moon, which meant that, even under the light gravity conditions prevailing on the satellite, there were many millions of tons of rock over their heads.

Frowning, Templin saw that there were strain-cracks on the tunnel walls—deep, long cracks that ran from floor to ceiling. They seemed to radiate from the point where the digging machine had been pinned down.

One of the workmen drifted over, watching Templin curiously. Templin glanced at the man, then turned to Culver. "Take a look at this," he ordered.

Culver looked indifferently. "Yeah. That's where the rock cracked and pinned down the machine."

"Uh-uh." Templin shook his head. "You've got the cart before the horse. Those cracks start at the mining machine. First the machine broke through, then the walls cracked."

Culver gaped at him through the transparent dome of his pressure suit. "So what?"

Templin grinned. "I don't know yet," he confessed. "But I aim to find out."

He picked up the case he had been carrying, opened it. Inside was a conglomeration of instruments—dials, meters, what looked like an old-fashioned portable radio, complete with earphones. These Templin disconnected, plugging the earphone lead into a socket on his collar-plate that led to his suit radio.

Culver's eyes narrowed curiously, then his expression cleared. "Oh, I get it," he said. "That's a sound-ranging gadget. You think—"

"I think maybe there's something wrong below," Templin cut in. "As I said yesterday, it looks to me as though there's a rock fault underneath here. That machine broke through the floor of the tunnel. When you consider how light it is, here on the Moon, that means that there was one damn thin shell of rock underneath it. Or else—well, I don't know what else it could be."

Culver laughed. "You'd better start thinking of something, Temp. That floor was solid; I know, because I handled the drilling on this gallery, and I was pretty careful not to let the Mark Seven come in until I'd sound-ranged the rock myself. Look—I've got the graphs back in the office. Come back and I'll show them to you."

Templin hesitated, then shook his head. "You might have made a mistake, Culver. I—I might as well tell you, I checked up on you. I looked over the sound-ranging reports last night. According to them, it's solid rock, all right—but still and all, the Mark Seven crashed through." He bent down and flipped the starting switch on his detection device. "Anyway, this will settle the question once and for all."

INSIDE THE satchel-like instrument, an electronic oscillator began sending out a steady beat, which was picked up by a sound-reflector and beamed out in a straight line. An electric "ear" in the machine listened for echoes, timed them against the sending impulse and in that way was able to locate very accurately the distance and direction of any flaw in the rock surrounding them.

The machine was sensitive enough to tell the difference between dry and oil-bearing strata of sand—it had been used for that work on Earth. And for it to recognize a cave in the solid rock of the Moon was child's play. So simple, and so hard to mistake, that Templin avoided the question of how the first reports, based on Culver's tests, could have been wrong. The machine could not be mistaken, Templin knew. Could the men who operated it have been treacherous?

Templin pointed the reflector of the instrument at the rock under the trapped Mark VII and reached for the control that would permit him to listen in on the telltale echoes from below.

Culver, watching Templin idly, saw the abrupt beginnings of a commotion behind him. The eight workmen who were clustered around the Mark VII suddenly dropped their tools and began to stampede toward them, puffy arms waving wildly and soundlessly.

"What the devil!" ejaculated Culver. Templin glanced up.

Then they felt it, too. Through the soles of their metal-shod feet they felt a growing vibration in the rock. Something was happening—something bad. They paused a second, then the workmen in their panicky flight came within range of their suit radios and they heard the words, *"Cave-in!"*

Templin straightened up. Ominously, the cracks in the wall were widening; there was a shuddering uneasiness in the feel of the rock floor beneath them that could mean only one thing. Somehow, the rockslide that had wrecked the Mark VII earlier was being repeated. Somewhere beneath their feet a hole in the rock was being filled—and it might well be their bodies that would fill it.

Cursing, Templin jumped aside to let the panic-stricken workmen dash by. Then, half-dragging the paralyzed Culver, he leaped for the monorail car to the surface. They were the last ones on, and they were just barely in time. The stampeding miners had touched the starting lever, and the monorail began to pick up speed under them as they scrambled aboard.

Looking dazedly behind as the monorail sped upward, Templin saw the roof of the tunnel shiver crazily, then drop down, obliterating the wrecked Mark VII from sight. Luckily, the cave-in spread no farther, but it was a frightful spectacle, that soundless, gigantic fall of rock.

And all the more so because, just as the roof came down on the digging machine, Templin saw a figure in pressure suit and opaque miner's helmet dash from the back of the machine to a sheltering cranny in the gallery wall. The man was trapped; even if there had been a way to stop the monorail and go back for a rescue try, there was no way of getting to him, through the thousands of cubic yards of rock that fell between, in time to save a life...

UP IN THE office, Templin was a caged tiger, raging as he paced back and forth. His stride was a ludicrous slow-motion shamble in the light gravity, but there was nothing ludicrous about his livid face.

He stopped and whirled on Culver. "Eight men down in that pit—and only seven of them got out! One of our men killed—half a million dollars worth of equipment buried—and why? Because some fool okayed the digging of a shaft directly over an underground cave!"

Culver shifted uncomfortably. "Wait a second, Temp," he begged. "I swear to you, there wasn't any cave there! Take a look at the sound-ranger graphs yourself."

Templin dragged in viciously on a cigarette. He exhaled a sharply cut-off plume of smoke, and when he answered his voice was under control again. "You're right enough, Culver," he said. "I've looked at the things. Only—there was a cave there, or else the miner wouldn't have fallen through. And how do you explain that?"

The door to the office opened and the personnel clerk stuck a worried head in. "I checked the rosters, Mr. Templin," he said.

Templin's jaw tensed in anticipation. "Who was missing?" he asked.

"That's the trouble, sir; no one is missing!"

"What!" Templin stared. "Look, Henkins, don't talk through your hat. There were eight miners down in that pit. Only seven came out. I saw one of them left behind, and there isn't a doubt in the world that he's still there dead. Who is it?"

The clerk said defensively, "I'm sorry, Mr. Templin. There are four men in the power plant, five guards patrolling the shaft and area and two men on liberty at Tycho City. Every one of them is checked and accounted for. Everybody else is right here in the building." He went on hastily, before Templin could explode, "But I took the liberty of talking to one of the miners who was down there with you, Mr. Templin. Like you, he said there were eight of them. But one man, he said, wasn't part of the regular crew. He didn't know who the odd man was. In fact..." Henkins hesitated. "...he thought it was *you!*"

"Me? Oh, for the good Lord's sake!" Templin glared disgustedly. "Look, Henkins, I don't care what your friend says—that man was part of the regular crew. At least he was a miner from this project—he had an opaque miner's helmet on; I saw it myself. You find out who he was, and don't come back here until you know."

"Yes, Mr. Templin," said Henkins despairingly, and he closed the door gently behind him.

Templin threw away his cigarette. "I would give five years' pay," he said moodily, "to be back on Mercury now. There I didn't have any troubles. All I had to worry about was keeping from falling into lava pits, and staying within sight of the ship."

Culver leaned back against the steel wall of the office. "Sounds fun," he said.

A buzzer sounded. Wearily Templin spoke into the teletone on his desk. "Hello, hello," he growled.

The voice that came out was the worried voice of Sam Bligh. It said, "Trouble, Templin. Something's happened to our energy reserves. The power leads are short-circuited. Can't tell what caused it yet—but it looks like sabotage."

THE GIANT parabolic mirrors were motionless as Culver and Templin approached them, pointed straight at the wide disk of the Earth hanging overhead. The two men glanced at them in passing, and hastened on to the low-roofed power building. Bligh was waiting for them inside. With a sweep of his arm he indicated the row of power meters that banked the wall.

"Look!" he said. "Every power pack we had in reserve—out. There isn't a watt of power in the project, except what's in the operating condensers." Templin followed the direction of his gesture, and saw that the needle on each meter rested against the "zero" pin.

"What happened?" Templin demanded.

Bligh shrugged helplessly. "See for yourself," he said. He pointed to a window looking down on the generating equipment buried beneath the power shack itself. "Those square contraptions on the right are the mercury-laminate power packs. The leads go from the generators to them; then we tap the packs for power as we need it. Somehow the leads were cut about five minutes ago. Right there."

Templin saw where the heavy insulated cables had been chopped off just at the mixing box that led to the packs. He looked at it for a long moment, eyes grim. "Sabotage. You're right, Bligh—that couldn't be an accident. Who was in here?"

Bligh shook his head. "No one—as far as I know. I saw no one. But there wasn't any special guard; there never is, here. Anyone in the project could have come in and done it."

Culver cut in, "How long will the power in the condenser last?"

"At our normal rate of use—half a day; if we conserve it—a week. By then the sun will be high enough so that the mirrors will be working again."

"Working again?" repeated Templin. "But the generators are working now, aren't they?"

Bligh hesitated. "Well—yes, but there isn't enough energy available to make much difference. The Moon takes twenty-eight days to revolve, you know—that means we have fourteen days of sunshine. That's when we get our power. At 'night'—when the sun's on the other side—we turn the mirrors on the Earth and pick up some reflected light, but it isn't enough to help very much."

Templin's face was gaunt in concentration. He said, "Order the project to cut down on power. Stretch out our reserves as much as you can, Bligh. Culver—get a crew ready on one of the freight rockets."

Culver raised his brows. "Where are we going, Temp?"

Templin said, "We're going to get some more power!"

CULVER SAID tightly over Templin's shoulder, "You realize, of course, that this is going to get us in serious trouble with the Security Patrol if they find out about it."

"We'll try to keep that from happening," said Templin. "Now don't bother me for a minute." His hands raced over the controls of the lumbering freight rocket. Underneath them lay the five-acre crater where they had crash-landed the day before after Olcott's attack. Templin killed the forward motion of the rocket with the nose jet, brought the nose up and set the ship down gently on the thundering fire of its tail rockets.

"Secure," he reported. "Are the crew in pressure suits? Good. Get them to work."

Culver sighed despondently and hurried off, shouting orders to the crew. Templin eased himself into his own suit. A hundred yards away lay the abandoned rocket-launching sites that had devastated a score of cities in the Three-Day War. Templin stepped out of the airlock and hastened after the group of pressure-suited men who were already investigating the ruined installation.

Culver waved to him. His voice over the radio was still disgusted as he said, "There's the pile, Temp; this is your last chance to back out of this crazy idea."

"We can't back out," Templin told him; "we need power. We can generate power with our own uranium, if we take this atomic pile back with us and start it up again. Maybe it's illegal, but it's the only way we can keep the mine going for the next week—and I'm taking the chance."

"Okay," said Culver. He gave orders to the men, who began to take the ten-year-old piece of equipment apart. In their ray-proof miners' suits, they were in no danger from the feeble radioactivity still left after the pile had exploded. But Templin was, and so was Culver; their suits were the lighter surface kind, and they had to keep their distance from the pile itself.

A nuclear-fission pile is an elaborate and clumsy piece of apparatus; it consists of many hundreds of cubes of graphite containing tiny pieces of uranium, stacked together, brick on brick, in the shape of a top. There are cadmium control-strips for checking the speed of the nuclear reaction, delicate instruments that keep tabs on what goes on inside the structure, heavy-metal neutron shields and gamma-ray barriers and enough other items to stock a warehouse.

Looking it over, Culver grumbled, "How the devil can we get that heap of junk into the rocket?"

"We'll get it in," promised Templin. He bent down clumsily to pick up a rock, crumbled it in his gauntleted fist. It was like chalk. "Soft," he said. "Burned up by atomic radiation."

Culver nodded inside his helmet. "Happened when the pile blew up, during the War."

"No. It's like this all over the Moon, as you ought to know by now." Templin tossed the powdered rock away and brushed it off his space-gauntlets. "There's something for you to figure out, Culver. I remember reading about it years ago, how the whole surface of the Moon shows that it must have been drenched with atomic rays a couple of thousand years ago. The shape of the craters—the fact that the surface air is all gone—the big cracks in the surface—it all adds up to show that there must have been a terrific atomic explosion here once."

He glanced again at where the miners were disassembling the pile. "I kind of think," he said slowly, "that that accounts for a lot of things here on the Moon. For one thing, it might explain what became of the Loonies, after they built their cities—and disappeared."

Culver said, "You mean that you think the Loonies had atomic power? And—and blew up the Moon with it?"

Templin shrugged, the gesture invisible inside the pressure suit. "Your guess," he said, "is as good as mine. Meanwhile, here comes the first load of graphite bricks. Let's give them a hand stowing it in the rocket."

ONCE THE JOB of setting up the stolen plutonium pile was complete, Templin began to feel as though he could see daylight ahead. There was a moment of hysterical tension when the pile first began to operate with uranium taken from the mine—a split-second of nervous fear as the cadmium safety rods were slowly withdrawn and the atomic fires within the pile began to kindle—but the safety controls still worked perfectly, and Templin drew a great breath of relief. An atomic explosion was bad enough anywhere...but here, in the works of a uranium mine where the ground was honeycombed with veins of raw atomic explosive, it was a thing to produce nightmares.

* * *

After two days of operation the power packs were being charged again and the mine was back in full-scale operation. Culver, seated in the office and looking at the day's production report, gloated to Templin, "Looks like we're in the clear now, Temp. Two hundred and fifty kilos of uranium in twenty-four hours—if we can keep that up for a month, maybe Terralune will begin to make some money on this place."

Templin blew smoke at the white metal ceiling. "Don't count your dividends before they're passed," he advised. "The Mark VII is still out of operation—we won't be able to start any new shafts until we get a replacement for it, so our production is limited to what we can get out of Gallery Eight. And besides—we took care of our power problem for the time being, all right, but what about taking care of the man who caused it?"

"Man who caused it?" repeated Culver.

"Yeah. Remember what Bligh said—that was sabotage. The leads were short-circuited deliberately."

"Oh." Culver's face fell. "We never found out who the missing miner was, either," he remembered. "Do you—"

THE TELETONE buzzed, interrupting him. When Templin answered, the voice that came out of the box was crisply efficient. "This is Lieutenant Carmer," it said. "Stand by for security check."

"Security check?" said Templin. "What the devil is that?"

The voice laughed grimly. "Tell you in just a moment," it promised. "Stand by. I'm on my way up."

The teletone clicked off. Templin faced Culver. "Well?" he demanded. "What is this?"

Culver said placatingly, "It's just a formality, Temp—at least, it always has been. The Security Patrol sends an officer around every month or so to every outpost on the Moon. All they do is ask a few questions and look to see if you've got any war-rocket launching equipment set up. The idea is to make sure that nobody installs rocket projectors to shoot at Earth with, as they did in the Three-Day War."

"Oh? And what about our plutonium pile?"

Culver said sorrowfully, "That bothers me, a little. But I don't think we need to worry, because we've got the thing in a cave and so far they've never looked in the caves."

"Well," said Templin, "all right. There's nothing we can do about it now, anyhow." He sat down at his desk and awaited his callers.

It only took a minute for the lieutenant to reach the office. But when the door opened Templin sat bolt upright, hardly believing his eyes.

The first man in was a trim, military-looking youth with lieutenant's bars on his shoulders. And following him, wearing the twin jets of a Security Patrol vice-commander, was the dark, heavy-set man with whom Templin had tangled in Hadley Dome, and whose ship had attacked them on the flight to the mine, Joe Olcott!

CHAPTER FOUR

THE LIEUTENANT closed the door behind his superior officer and marched up to Templin. He dropped an ethergram form on Templin's desk. "My inspection orders," he said crisply. "Better look them over and see they're all right, I take it that you're the new boss around here."

Templin took his eyes off Olcott with difficulty. To the lieutenant he said non-committally, "I run the mine, yes. Name's Templin. This is Jim Culver, works superintendent."

The lieutenant relaxed a shade. "We've met," he acknowledged, nodding to Culver. "I'm Lieutenant Carmer, and this is Commander Olcott."

Templin said dryly, "I've met Mr. Olcott. Twice—although somewhat informally."

Olcott growled, "Never mind that; we're here on business."

"What sort of business?"

The lieutenant said hesitantly, "There has been a complaint made against you, Mr. Templin—a report of a violation of security regulations."

"Violation? What violation?" Templin reached casually for another cigarette as he spoke, but his senses were alert. This was the man with whom he had had trouble twice before; it looked like a third dose was in the offing.

Carmer looked at Joe Olcott before he spoke. "Plutonium, Mr. Templin," he said.

Culver coughed spasmodically. Templin said, "I see. Well, of course you can't take any chances, Lieutenant. Absurd as it is, you'd better investigate the report." To Culver he said, "Go up to the quarters and pick out two guides for them, Culver. They'll want to see our whole layout here; maybe you'd better go along too."

Culver nodded, his face full of trouble. "Okay, Temp," he said dismally, and went out.

Templin picked up the ether-grammed orders and read them carefully, stalling for time. They said nothing but what he already knew; they were typical military orders authorizing a party of two officers to inspect the Terralune Projects mine at Hyginus Cleft. He put it down carefully.

He got up. "Excuse me for a while," he said. "Culver will take care of you, and I've got a load of ore coming out to check. If you have any questions, I'll see you before you leave."

Olcott guffawed abruptly. "You bet you will," he sniggered, but he caught Templin's mild eyes and the laughter went out of him. "Go ahead," he said. "We'll see you, all right."

Templin took his time about leaving. At the door he said, "There are cigarettes on the desk; help yourselves," Then he closed the door gently behind him…and at once was galvanized into action. He raced to the metal climbing pole to the quarters on the upper level, swarmed up it at top speed and bounded down the galleyway, looking for Culver. He found Culver and two miners coming out of one of the rooms; he stopped them, took Culver aside.

"I need half an hour," he said. "Can you keep them away from the pile that long? After that—I'll be ready."

Culver said hesitantly, "I guess so. But what's the deal, Temp?"

"You'll find out," Templin promised. "Get going!"

TEMPLIN took three men and got them into pressure suits in a hurry. They didn't even take time to pump air out of the pressure chamber; as soon as the inner door was sealed, Templin slammed down the emergency release and the outer door popped open. The four of them were almost blasted out of the lock by the sudden rush of air under normal pressure expanding into the vacuum outside. It was a waste of precious oxygen—but Templin was in a hurry.

The stars outside were incandescent pinpoints in the ebony sky. Off to the west the tops of the mountains were blinding bright in the sun, but it was still night at the mine and the huge Earth hung in the sky overhead.

They leaped across the jagged rock, heading toward the abandoned shaft in which lay the plutonium pile Templin had stolen. As they passed the gleaming mirrors of the solar energy collectors Templin glanced at them and swore to himself. Without the pile's power to recharge their power-packs they were dependent on the feeble trickle of Earthshine for all their power—far less than the elaborate power-thirsty equipment of the mine needed. But there was no help for it. Perhaps when Olcott and the security lieutenant had gone, they could revive the pile again and resume mining operations; until then, there would be no power, and mining operations would stop.

Hastily he set two of the men to digging up and re-channeling the leads to the power dome. Templin and the other man scuttled down into the yawning black shaft.

In the darting light of his helmet lamp he stared around, calculating the risks for the job in hand. The pile had to be concealed; the only way to conceal it was to blast the mouth of the tunnel shut. The pile itself was made of sturdy stuff, of course, with its ray-proof shielding and solid construction. But certainly operation of the pile would have to stop while Olcott and the lieutenant were in the vicinity, for the tiny portable Geiger counters they carried would surely detect the presence of a working atomic pile, no matter how thick and thorough the shielding.

And once a plutonium pile was stopped, it took hours to coax the nuclear reaction back to life. Any attempt to do it in a hurry would mean atomic explosion.

Templin signaled to the workman, not daring to use his radio, and the two of them tackled the cadmium-metal dampers that protruded from the squat bulk of the pile. Thrust in as far as they would go, they soaked up the flow of neutrons; slowing down the atomic reaction until, like a forest fire cooled by cascading rain, the raging atomic fires flickered and went out. The reaction was stopped. The spinning gas turbines of the heat exchanger slowed and halted; the current generator stopped revolving. The atomic pile was dead.

On the surface, Templin knew, the current supply for the whole mining area was being shifted to the solar-energy reserves. The lights would flicker a little; then, as the automatic selector switches tapped the power packs, they would go back on—a little dimmer, no doubt.

Templin groaned regretfully and gestured to the other miner, who was throwing a heavy sheet-metal hook over the exposed moving part of the generator. They hurried up and out to the surface.

Templin pulled a detonation-bomb from the cluster he had hung at his waist and, carefully gauging the distance, tossed it down the shaft. It struck a wall, rolled a dozen yards.

Then Templin flung himself away from the mouth of the shaft, dragging the other man with him. The bomb went off.

There was a flare of light and through the soles of their spacemen's boots they felt the vibration, but there was no sound. Templin saw a flat area of rock bulge noiselessly upward, then collapse. The entrance was sealed.

Grim-faced, Templin turned to await the coming of the inspection party. He had done all that could be done.

A MINER, apparently one of the two who had been re-locating the power leads, was standing nearby. Templin said curtly into the radio, "If you're finished, get back to the quarters." The man hesitated, then waved and moved slowly off.

Looking at the lights of the mine buildings, Templin could see that they were less bright now than before. Around the buildings small clusters of tinier lights were moving—the helmet lamps of pressure-suited men.

Looking close, Templin saw that three of the smaller lights were coming toward him—Culver, Olcott and the security lieutenant, he was sure. He gestured to his helper to keep out of sight and, in great swooping strides, he bounded toward the three lights.

As he got closer he could see them fairly clearly in the reddish light reflected from Earth overhead. They were the three he had expected, sure enough; they wore the clear, transparent helmets of surface Moon-dwellers, not the cloudy ray-opaque shields of the miners. He greeted them through his radio as casually as he could. "Find any plutonium?" he inquired amiably.

Even in the dim light he could Olcott's face contort in a snarl. "You know damn well we didn't," said Olcott. "But I know it's here; if I didn't have to be in Hadley Dome in two hours I'd stay right here until I found it!"

Templin spread his hands. "Next time, bring your lunch," he said.

The lieutenant spoke up. "We felt blasting going on, Templin," he said. "What was it?"

"Opening a shaft," Templin explained carefully; "we're in the mining business here, you know."

Olcott said, "Never mind that. Where are you getting your power?"

Templin looked at him curiously. "Solar radiation," he said. "Where else?"

"Liar!" spat Olcott. "You know that your sun-generators broke down! You don't have enough reserves to carry you through the night—" He broke off as he caught Templin's eye.

"Yes," said Templin softly, "I know we don't have enough reserves. But tell me, how did *you* know it?"

Olcott hesitated. Then, aggressively, "We—the Security Patrol has its ways of finding things out," he said. "Anyway, that doesn't matter. I've been tracing your power lines out from the mine; if they end in solar generators, I'll admit we were wrong. I'm betting they end in a plutonium pile."

Templin nodded. "Fair enough," he said. "Let's follow the lines."

OLCOTT'S rage when they came to the banks of light-gathering mirrors and photocells knew no bounds. "What the devil, Templin," he raged. "What are you trying to put over on us? Look at your power gauges—you haven't enough juice left there to electrocute a fly! Your reserves are way down—the only intake is a couple of hundred amps from the reflected Earthshine—and you're trying to make us think you run the whole mine on it!"

Templin shrugged. "We're very economical of power," he said. "Go around turning lights out after us, and that sort of thing."

The Lieutenant had the misfortune to chuckle. Olcott turned on him, anger shining on his face. Templin stood back to watch the fireworks. Then...Olcott seemed, all of a sudden, to calm down.

He glanced at one of the miners, who had come up to join them, then at Templin. He pointed to the spot where Templin had just touched off the blast concealing the pile.

"What's over there?" he demanded triumphantly.

Templin froze. "Over where?" he stalled; but he knew it was a waste of time.

"Under that blasted rock," crowed Olcott. "You know what I'm talking about! Where you just blasted in the tunnel over your contraband plute pile!"

Templin, dazed and incredulous, stumbled back a step. How had Olcott stumbled on the secret? Templin could have sworn that a moment ago Olcott was completely in the dark—and yet—

Olcott snarled to the lieutenant, "Arrest that man! He's got a plutonium pile going in violation of security regulations!"

Hesitantly the lieutenant looked at his superior officer, then at Templin. He stepped tentatively toward Templin, arm outstretched to grab him...

Templin took a lightning-swift split-second to make up his mind, then he acted. He was between the other three men and the mine buildings. Beyond them was the Moon, millions of square miles of desolation. It was his only chance.

Templin plunged through the group, catching them by surprise and scattering them like giant slow-motion ninepins. Leaning far forward to get the maximum thrust and speed from his feet, he raced ahead, spanning twenty-foot pits and crevasses, heading for a crater edge where the rocks were particularly jagged and contorted. He was a hundred yards away, and going fast, before the three men could recover from their astonishment.

Then the first explosion blossomed soundlessly on a jagged precipice to his right.

It was the lieutenant's rocket pistol, for Olcott had none of his own—but Templin knew that it was the fat man's hand that was firing at him. Templin zigzagged frantically. Soundless explosions burst around him, but Olcott's aim was poor, and he wasn't touched.

Then Templin was behind the crater wall. He crashed into a rock outcrop with a jolt that sent him reeling and made him fear, for a second, that he had punctured the airtightness of his helmet. But he hurried on, ran lightly for a hundred yards parallel to the wall, found a jet-black shadow at the base of a monolith of rock and crouched there, waiting.

There was no hiss of escaping air; his suit was still intact. After a moment he saw the lights of two men crossing the crater wall. They bobbed around for long minutes, searching for Templin. But there was too much of the Moon, too many sheltering hollows and impenetrable darknesses. After a bit they turned and went back toward the mine.

Templin gave them an extra five minutes for good measure. Then he cautiously crawled out of his hiding place and peered over the ridge.

No one was in sight, all the way to the mine buildings. He watched the lights of the buildings for a while, his face drawn with worry. The events of the last few moments had happened too rapidly to give him a chance to realize how bad a spot he was in. Now it was all coming to him. He had made a desperate gamble when he took the plutonium pile—and lost.

He stood there for several minutes, thinking out his position and what he had to do.

Then he saw something that gave him an answer to one of his problems, at least.

There was a sudden swelling burst of ruddy light that bloomed beyond the mine buildings, in the flat place where rocket ships landed. It got brighter, became white, then rose and lengthened into a sharp-pointed plume that climbed toward the tiny, bright stars overhead. It was the drive-jet off a rocket, taking off. Templin watched the flame level off, hurtle along at top speed in the direction of Tycho Crater.

It was the jet that had brought Olcott and the lieutenant. Templin was sure. They were going—but they would be back.

He hadn't much time. And he had a lot to do.

TAKING NO chances, Templin kept in the cover of the jagged rocks as he approached the dome. A few hundred yards from it he saw a pressure-suited figure moving toward him. He stood motionless in indecision for a moment, until he saw that the helmet on the figure was milkily opaque. A miner's helmet.

Templin stood up and beckoned to the figure. When it was within a few yards he said, "Have the Security Patrol officers gone?"

The miner stopped. Templin was conscious of invisible eyes regarding him through the one-way vision of the helmet. Then he heard a voice say, "Oh, it's you, Templin. I was wondering where you were."

Templin thought that there was something curious about the voice—not an accent, but a definite peculiarity of speech that he couldn't recognize. Almost as though the man were speaking a foreign language—

Templin glanced toward the dome and dismissed the thought. Someone was coming toward them; he had to make sure of his ground. He asked, "That rocket I saw— was that the Security Patrol? Have they both gone?"

"Yes."

"Fine!" Templin exulted. "Where's Culver, then?"

The figure in the spacesuit gestured. Templin, following the pointing arm, saw the man who was coming toward them. "Thanks," he said, and raced to meet Culver, who was quartering off toward the power plant. Templin intercepted him only a short distance from the main building.

"Culver," he said urgently, "come into the dome. I've not got much time, so I've got to move fast. When Olcott and—" He broke off, staring. Culver was looking at him, his expression visibly puzzled even in the twilight, his mouth moving but no sound coming over the radio.

"What's the matter?" Templin demanded. Culver just stared. "Ahh," growled Templin, "your radio is broken. Come on!" He half-dragged Culver the remaining short distance to the dome. They climbed into the airlock. Templin closed the outer pressure doors and touched the valve that flooded the chamber with air. Before they were out of the lock Templin had his helmet off, was motioning to Culver to do likewise.

"What the devil was the matter with your radio?" he demanded.

"Nothing," said Culver in surprise. "It's yours that doesn't work."

"Well—never mind. Anyway, what happened to Olcott?"

"Took off for Tycho. Gone for a posse to hunt for you, I guess."

"Why didn't they radio for help?"

Culver grinned a little self-consciously. "That was me," he explained. "I—I told them we didn't have enough juice to run the radio. They didn't like it, but there wasn't anything they could do. We don't have very much power, and that's a fact."

Templin laughed. "Good boy," he said. "All right. Here's what I want to do. Olcott said he was going to Hadley Dome. I want to be there when he gets there. I think it's time for a showdown."

Culver looked forlorn, but all he said was, "I'll get a rocket ready." He went to the teletone in the anteroom, gave orders to the ground crew of the rockets. To Templin he said, "Let's go outside."

Templin nodded and got ready to put his helmet back on. As he was lifting it over his head something caught his eye.

"What the devil!" he said. "Hey, Culver. Take a look."

Culver looked. At the base of the helmet was a metal lug to which was fastened one of the radio leads. But the lug was snapped off clean; bright metal showed where it had connected with the helmet itself. The radio was broken.

Culver said in self-satisfaction, "Told you so, Temp; it was broken before, when I tried to talk to you outside."

Templin said thoughtfully, "Maybe so. Might have broken when I ran into that rock out at the crater—no! It couldn't have been broken. I was talking to a miner over it just before I met you."

"What miner?"

Templin stared at him. "Why, the one who left the building just before you did."

Culver shook his head. "Look, Temp," he said. "I had all hands in here when Olcott and the lieutenant took off. And I was the first one out of the place afterwards. There wasn't any miner."

TEMPLIN STOOD rooted in astonishment for a moment. Then he blinked. "I talked to somebody," he growled. "Listen, I've got twenty minutes or so before I have to take off. Let's go out and take a look for this miner!"

Culver answered by reaching for a suit. Templin picked another helmet with radio tap intact and put it on; they trotted into the pressure lock and let themselves out the other side.

Templin waved. "That's where I saw him." But there was no sign of the "miner".

Templin led off toward where the pressure-suited figure had seemed to be heading, out toward the old Loonie city. They scoured the jagged Moonscape, separating to the limit of their radio-contact range, investigating every peak and crater.

Then Culver's voice crackled in Templin's ear. "Look out there!" it said. "At the base of that rock pyramid!"

Templin looked. His heart gave a bound. Something was moving, something that glinted metallically and jogged in erratic fashion across the rock, going away from them.

"That's it!" said Templin. "It's heading toward the Loonie city. Come on—maybe we can head him off!"

The thing went out of sight behind an outcropping of rock, and Templin and Culver raced toward it. It was a good quarter mile away, right at the fringe of the Loonie city itself. It took them precious minutes to get there, more minutes before they found what they sought.

Then Templin saw it, lying on the naked rock. "Culver!" he whooped. "Got it!"

They approached cautiously. The figure lay motionless, face down at the entrance to one of the deserted moon warrens.

Templin snarled angrily, "Okay, whoever you are! Get up and start answering questions!"

There was no movement from the figure. After a second Culver leaned over to inspect it, then glanced puzzledly at Templin. "Dead?" he ventured.

Templin scowled and thrust a foot under the spacesuit, heaved on it to roll it over.

To his surprise, the force of his thrust sent the thing flying into the air like a football at the kick. Its lightness was incredible. They stared at it open-mouthed as it floated in a high parabola. As it came down they raced to it, picked it up.

The helmet fell off as they were handling it. Culver gasped in wonder.

There was no one in the suit!

Templin said, "Good lord, Culver, he—he took the suit off! But there isn't any air. He would have died!"

Culver nodded soberly. "Temp," he said in an awed voice, "just *what* do you suppose was wearing that suit?"

CHAPTER FIVE

TEMPLIN jockeyed the little jet-ship down to a stem landing at the entrance to Hadley Dome, so close to the Dome itself that the pressure-chamber attendant met him with a glare. But one look at Templin's steel-hard face toned down the glare, and all the man said, very mildly, was, "You were a little close to the Dome, sir. Might cause an accident."

Templin looked at him frigidly. "If anything happens to this rat-hole," he said, "it won't be an accident. Out of my way."

He mounted the wide basalt stair to Level Nine and pounded Ellen Bishop's door. A timid maid peeped out at Templin and said, "Miss Bishop is upstairs in the game room, sir. Shall I call her on the Dome phone and tell her you're here?"

"Tell her myself," said Templin. He spun around and climbed the remaining flight of stairs to the top of Hadley Dome.

He was in a marble-paved chamber where a gentle fountain danced a slow watery waltz. To his right was Hadley Dome's tiny observatory, where small telescopes watched the face of the Earth day and night. Directly ahead lay the game room, chief attraction of Hadley Dome for its wealthy patrons and a source of large-scale revenue to the billionaire syndicate that owned the Dome.

For Earthly laws did not exist on Hadley Dome; the simple military code that governed the Moon enforced the common law, and certain security regulations, and nothing else. Crimes of violence came under the jurisdiction of the international Security Patrol, but there was no law regulating drugs, alcohol, morals—or gambling. And it was for gambling in particular that the Dome had become famous.

Templin hesitated at the threshold of the game room and stared around for Ellen Bishop. Contemptuously, his eyes roved over the clustered knots of thrill-seekers. There were fewer than fifty persons in the room, yet he could see that gigantic sums of money were changing hands. At the roulette table nearest him a lean, tired-looking croupier was raking in glittering chips of synthetic diamond and ruby. Each chip was worth a hundred dollars or more…and there were scores of chips in the pile.

Templin took his eyes off the sight to peer around for Olcott. The man was not in the room, and Templin mentally thanked his gods.

But at the far end, standing with her back to the play and looking out a window on the blinding vista of sun-tortured rock that was the Sea of Serenity, was Ellen Bishop, all alone.

Templin walked up behind her, gently touched her on the shoulder. The girl started and spun round like a released torsion coil.

"Templin!" she gasped. "You startled me."

Templin chuckled comfortably. "Sorry," he said, "Have you seen Olcott?"

"Why, no. I don't think he's in the Dome. But, Temp—what is the trouble at Hyginus? Culver radioed that the Security Patrol was after you for something! What is it?"

"Plenty of trouble," Templin admitted soberly. "And I only know one way out of it. Look, Ellen—don't ask questions right now; there are too many people around here, with too many ears. And I want you to do something."

He glanced around the room, selected a dice table that had a good view of the door. "Let's risk a few dollars," he suggested. "I have a feeling that this is my lucky night!"

TEMPLIN played cautiously, for the stakes were too high for any man on a salary to afford. But by carefully betting against the dice and controlling the impulse to pyramid his winnings, he managed to stay a few chips ahead of the game.

Ellen, scorning to play, was fuming beside him. She said in a vicious whisper, "Temp, this is the most idiotic thing I ever heard of! Don't you know that the Patrol is after you? Olcott comes here every night; if he sees you—it's all up!"

Templin grinned. "Patience," he said. "I know what I'm doing. Give you six to five that the man doesn't make his eight."

Ellen tossed her head. "Too bad," said Templin. "I would have won." The dice passed to Templin; he made one point, picked up his winnings, threw another and sevened out. He sighed and waited expectantly for the man beside him to bet.

Then—he saw what he was waiting for.

Joe Olcott appeared briefly in the door of the gambling salon. Templin spotted him at once and carefully took the opportunity to light a cigarette, screening most of his down-turned face with his hand. But it was an unnecessary precaution; Olcott was looking for someone else, a chubby little servile-looking man, who trotted up to him as soon as the big man appeared in the door. There was a brief whispered conversation, then Olcott and the chubby one disappeared.

Templin waited thirty seconds after they left. "I knew it," he exulted. "Olcott said he was coming back here—and I know why! Come on, Ellen—I want to see where he's going."

Ellen stuttered protest but Templin dragged her out. They followed the other two into the hall and saw that the elevator indicator showed that the cage was on its way down. "They're on it," said Templin. "Come on—stairs are faster." He led the complaining girl clown the long basalt stairways at a precipitous pace. She was exhausted, and even Templin was breathing hard, when they rounded the landing to come to the last flight of stairs. He slowed down abruptly, and they carefully peeked into the lobby of Hadley Dome before coming into sight.

Olcott's chubby companion had parted from him, was disappearing down a long corridor that led to the Dome's radio room. Olcott himself was putting on a pressure suit, preparatory to going outside.

Templin halted, concealed by the high balustrade of the stair. He nodded sharply, to himself. "This is it, Ellen," he said to the girl. "Something has been going on—something so fantastic that I hardly dare speak of it, far beyond anything we've dreamed of. But I think I know what it is...and the way Olcott is acting makes me surer of it every minute."

"What are you talking about?" demanded the girl.

Templin laughed. "You'll see," he promised. "Meanwhile, Olcott's on his way to a certain place that I want very much to see. I'm going after him; you stay here."

Ellen Bishop stamped a foot. "I'm going along!" she said.

Templin shook his head. "Uh-uh. You're not—that's final. When this is over I'll be working for you again—but right now I'm the boss. And you're staying here."

HE LEFT her fuming and went out through the pressure chamber, hastily tugging on the suit he had reclaimed from the attendant. Templin had barely sealed the helmet when the outer door opened, and vacuum sucked at him.

He blinked painfully, staggered by the shock, as he stepped out into the blinding fierce sun. In the days that had passed since last Templin was at Hadley Dome, the Moon's slow circling of the Earth had brought the Dome into direct sunlight, agonizingly bright—hot enough to warm the icy rock far above the boiling point of water overnight. The helmet of his suit, even stopped down as far as the polarizing device would go, still could not keep out enough of that raging radiation to make it really comfortable. But after a few moments the worst of it passed, and he could see again.

Templin stared around for Olcott, confident that he wouldn't see him...and he did not. Olcott was not among the ships parked outside the Dome. Olcott was out of sight around the Dome's bulk; Templin followed and stared out over the heat-sodden Sea of Serenity.

Olcott's figure, bloated and forbidding-looking in the pressure suit, was bounding clumsily down the long slope of Mount Hadley, going in the general direction of a small crater, miles off across the tortured rocky Sea. Templin stared at the crater thoughtfully for a second. Then he remembered its name.

"Linne," he said underneath his breath. "Yes!" With a sudden upsurge at the heart he recalled the story of Linne Crater—site of one of the biggest and least-dilapidated Lunarian cities—the so-called "Vanishing Crater" of the Nineteenth Century.

Templin nodded soberly to himself, but wasted no more time in contemplation. Already Olcott was almost out of sight, his bloated figure visible only when he leaped over a crevasse or surmounted a plateau. It would be easy enough to lose him in this jagged, sun-drenched waste, Templin knew...so he hurried after the other man.

Templin remembered the story of Linne, always an enigma to Moon-gazers. It was Linne that, little more than a century before, had been reported by Earthly astronomers as having disappeared...then, a few years later in 1870, it had been discovered again in the low-power telescopes of the period—but with important changes in its shape.

What—Templin wondered abstractly—did those changes in its shape mean?

* * *

Obviously, Linne was their goal. It lay directly ahead in the path Olcott had taken, a good thirty miles away—across the roughest, most impassable kind of terrain that existed anywhere in the universe men traversed. A good three-day hike on Earth, it was only about an hour's time away on foot, on the light-gravitied surface of the Moon. But it would be an hour of sustained, strenuous exertion, and Templin gave all his concentration to the task of getting there.

A mile farther on, Templin glanced up as he cleared a hundred-foot-deep crevasse. Olcott's figure was nowhere to be seen.

Templin halted, a frown on his lean face. The fat man couldn't have reached the shelter of Linne crater yet—or could he? Had Linne been a wrong guess, after all—was Olcott's destination some place between?

Templin shrugged. Certainly Olcott was out of sight; it behooved Templin to get moving, to try to catch up.

He put his full strength into a powerful leg-thrust that sent him hurtling across a ravine and down into a shallow depression on the other side of it. As he balanced himself for the next leap...

Disaster struck.

OUT OF THE corner of his eye, Templin saw a flicker of motion. A sprawling, spread-eagled figure in a pressure suit was sailing down on him from the lee of a small crater nearby; and from one of the outstretched hands glittered a brilliant, diamond-like reflection of sunlight on steel.

It was a spaceman's knife, and the man who bore it, Templin knew, was Olcott.

Templin writhed aside and out of the way of the knife, but the flailing legs of Olcott caught him and knocked him down. Templin rolled like a ball, landed on his feet facing the other man. Olcott's face behind the clouded semiopacity of the helmet was contorted in hatred, and the long knife in his hand was a murderous instrument as he leaped toward Templin again.

Templin paused a moment, irresolute. Olcott didn't have a gun with him, he saw; if Templin chose, he could take to his heels and Olcott wouldn't have a chance in the world of catching him. But something within Templin would never let him run from a battle...with scarcely a second's hesitation, he grabbed for the dirk at his own belt and faced his antagonist. If it was fight that Olcott was after, he would give it to the man.

The two closed warily, eyes alert for the slightest weakness on the other's part. Strange, deadly battle, these two humans on the seared face of the Moon! In an age of fantastic technological advance, it was to the knife, after all, that humanity had returned for killing. For nothing could be more deadly than a single tiny rent made by one of these razor-sharp space knives in the puffed pressure suit of an enemy. At the tiniest slit the air would flood out, quick as bomb-flash, and the body of the man inside would burst in horrid soundless explosion as the pressures within it sought to expand into the vacuum.

Olcott drove a wicked thrust at Templin's mid-section, which the bigger man parried with his steel space-gauntlet. He dodged and let the chunky killer jerk free. Templin's mind was clear, not masked by blinding rage: he would kill Olcott if he had to, yes—but, if possible, Templin would somehow disarm the other and keep him alive.

Olcott feinted to the left, sidestepped and came in with a shoulder-high lunge. Templin shifted lightly away, then seized his chance; he ducked, dived inside Olcott's murderous thrust, drove against him with the solid shoulder of his pressure suit. The heavy-set man puffed soundlessly, the wind knocked out of him, as he spun away from the blow. Templin followed up with a sledgehammer blow to the forearm; the knife flew out of Olcott's hand, and Templin pounced.

He bore the other man down by sheer weight and impact, knelt on his chest, knife pressed against the bulge of the pressure suit just where it joined the collar. With his free hand he flicked on his helmet radio and said, "Give up, Olcott. You're licked and you know it."

Olcott's face was strained and suddenly as pale as the disk of the Moon itself. He licked his lips. "All—all right," he croaked. "Take that knife away, for the love of heaven!"

Templin looked at him searchingly, then nodded and stood up.

"Get up," he ordered. Olcott sullenly pushed himself up on one arm. Then, abruptly, a flash of pain streaked across his face. "My leg!" he groaned. "Damn you, Templin, you've broken it!"

Templin frowned and moved toward him cautiously. He bent to look at the leg, but in the shrouding bulkiness of the air-filled pressure suit there was no way for him to tell if Olcott was lying. He said, "Try and get up."

Olcott winced and shook his head. "I can't," he said, "It's broken."

Templin bent closer, suspiciously. "Looks all right to me—" he started to say. Then he realized his mistake—but too late to do him any good.

Olcott's other leg came up with the swiftness of a striking snake, drew back and lashed out in a vicious kick that caught Templin full in the ribs, sent him hurtling helplessly a dozen yards back. He wind-milled his arms, trying to regain his balance…but he had no chance, for at once the ground slid away from under him as he reeled backward into the yawning 500-foot crevasse, and down!

LITHE AS a cat, Templin twisted his body around in space to land on his feet. The fall was agonizingly slow, but he still possessed all the mass, if not the weight, of his two hundred-pound body, and if he struck on his helmet it would mean death.

He landed feet-first. The impact was bone shattering, but his space-trained leg muscles had time to flex and cushion the shock. As it was, he blacked out for a moment, and came to again to looking up into a blinding sun overhead that silhouetted the head and shoulders of Olcott, peering down at him.

They looked at each other for a long moment. Then Templin heard the crackle of Olcott's voice in his helmet, and realized with a start that his radio was still working. "A hero," jeered Olcott. "Following after me single-handed. Sorry I couldn't let you come along with me."

Templin was silent.

"I'd like to ask you questions," Olcott continued, "but right now I haven't got time; I've got some urgent affairs to take care of."

"In Linne," said Templin. "I know, go ahead, Olcott. I'll see you there."

Olcott's figure was quite motionless for a second. Then, "No," he said, "I don't think you will." And his head disappeared over the lip of the crevasse.

*   *   *

Templin had just time enough to wonder what Olcott was up to…when he found out.

A giant, jagged boulder came hurtling down in slow motion from the edge of the chasm.

Slowly as it fell, Templin had just time enough to get out of its way before it struck. It landed with a shattering vibration that he felt through the soles of his feet, sending up splinters of jagged rock that splattered off his helmet and pressure suit. And it was followed by another, and a third, coming down like a giant deadly hail in slow motion.

Then Olcott's head reappeared, to see what the results of his handiwork has been.

Templin, crouched against a boulder just like the ones that had rained down, had sense enough to play dead. He stared up at Olcott with murder in his heart, disciplining himself, forcing himself not to move. For a long moment Olcott looked down.

Then Templin saw an astonishing thing.

Against the far wall of the crevasse, just below Olcott's head, a flare of light burst out, and almost at once a second, a few yards away.

Templin could see Olcott leap in astonishment, jerk upright and stare in the direction of Hadley Dome.

Someone was shooting a rocket pistol at Olcott. But whom?

Whoever the person was, he was a friend in deed to Steve Templin. Olcott scrambled erect and disappeared; Templin waited cautiously for a long moment, but he didn't come back. Templin's unknown friend had driven the other man off, forced him to flee in the direction of the Loonie city at Linne Crater.

Templin, hardly believing in his luck, stood up. For several seconds he stood staring at the lip of the cleft, waiting to see what would happen.

A moment later a new helmet poked over the side of the chasm nearest Hadley Dome. Templin peered up in astonishment. It looked like—It was.

The voice in his helmet was entirely familiar. "Oh, Temp, you utter idiot," it said despairingly. "Are you all right?"

It was Ellen Bishop. "Bless your heart," said Templin feelingly. "Of course I'm all right. Stand by to give me a hand—I'm coming up!"

CHAPTER SIX

IT WASN'T easy, but Templin finally managed to scramble out of the crevasse—after loping nearly half a mile along the bottom of it, to where the sides were less precipitous. Ellen Bishop, following his progress from above, was there to meet him as he clambered over the edge.

Remembering the genuine anxiety in her voice as it had come over the radio, he peered curiously at her face; but behind the shading helmet it was hard to read expressions. He smiled.

"You win another Girl Scout merit badge," he observed. "Whatever made you show up in the nick of time like that?"

Ellen's face colored slightly. "I was watching you," she said defiantly. "There's a spotting telescope in the Observatory at Hadley Dome and—well, I was worried about you. I went up and watched. I saw Olcott stop and look around, and then hide…so I figured out that he'd seen you. It looked like an ambush. And of course, you were such a big fool that you didn't take a rocket gun along with you."

"Couldn't afford to," Templin apologized. "Olcott's still in the Security Patrol—I didn't want to be caught following him with a gun tucked in my belt. Besides, he didn't have one himself."

"He had something," Ellen said.

"Or did you just go down in that crevasse to look for edelweiss?"

Templin coughed. "Well," he said ambiguously. "As long as you're here, you might as well come the rest of the way." He craned his neck in the direction of the Loonie city, mockingly near now. Olcott was not in sight.

"Come on," he offered. "Keep out of trouble, though. Olcott went a little too far when he jumped me. He can't turn back any more...and that means he's desperate."

The girl nodded. Side by side they drove on toward the solitary crater of Linne, alone in the middle of the Mare Serenitatis. Once Templin thought he saw Olcott's figure on top of a peak, watching them. But it didn't reappear, and he decided he had been mistaken...

They loped into the ancient city of the long-dead lunar race, Templin in the lead but the girl only a hair's-breadth behind. In the shadow of a giant ruined tower Templin gestured, and they came to a stop.

He switched off the transmitter of his helmet radio, motioned to the girl to do the same. When, somewhat puzzled, she obeyed, he leaned close to her, touching helmets.

"Keep your radio off!" he yelled, and the vibration carried his voice from his helmet to hers. "This is where Olcott's outfit hides out, whoever they are. If they hear our radios it'll be trouble."

ELLEN NODDED, and the two of them advanced down the broad street of the ravished Lunarian metropolis. Glancing at the shattered buildings all about them, Templin found his mind dwelling on the peculiar tragedy of the Moon's former inhabitants, who had risen from the animal, developed a massive civilization, had seen it wiped out into nothingness.

Ellen shuddered and moved closer to Templin. He understood her feeling; even to him, the city seemed haunted. The light of the giant sun that hung overhead was blinding; yet he found himself becoming jittery, seeing strange imaginary shapes that twisted and contorted in the utterly black shadows cast by the ruined walls.

They circled a shattered Coliseum, looking warily into every crevice, when Templin felt Ellen's gauntleted hand on his shoulder. He looked at her and touched helmets. Her face was worried. "Someone's watching us, Temp," she said positively, her voice metallic as it was transmitted by the helmets. "I feel eyes."

"Where?"

"How do I know? In that big round building we just passed, I think. It feels exactly as if they keep going around and around the building at the same time we do, always staying on the far side from us."

Templin considered. "Let's look," he said. "You go one way, I'll go the other. We'll meet on the other side."

"Oh, Temp!"

"Don't be frightened, Ellen. You have your gun—and I can take care of myself with my space knife."

Her lip trembled. "All right," she said. Templin watched her start off. She had drawn the gun and was holding it ready as she walked.

Templin went clockwise around the building, moving slowly and carefully, his hand always poised near the dirk at his belt. Almost anything might be lurking in the cavernous hollows in these old buildings. Olcott, he felt quite sure, was lurking somewhere nearby—and so were his mysterious friends. Templin stepped over a fallen carven pillar—strange ornamentation of curious serpentine beasts and almost-human figures straining toward the sky was on it—and froze as he thought he saw a flicker of motion out of the corner of his eye. But it was not repeated, and after a moment he went on.

He was clear back to his starting point before he realized that Ellen had disappeared.

TEMPLIN SWORE in the silence. There was no doubt about it. He had traveled completely around the circular building, and Ellen was gone.

He hesitated a second, feeling the forces of mystery gathering about him as they had about Ellen, then grimly dismissed the fantasy from his mind. There had to be a way of finding Ellen again...and at once.

His mind coldly alert, he circled the ancient Lunarian structure once more. Ellen was not in sight.

Templin stood still, thinking it over. Cautiously he retraced his tracks, eyes fixed on the soft Lunarian rock beneath him.

Fifteen yards away, he saw the marks of a scuffle on the ray-charred rock. Heavy space boots had been dragged there, making deep, protesting scars. Ellen.

Templin swore soundlessly and loosened his space knife in its scabbard. He stared up at the ruined Loonie temple. A crumbled arch was before him; inside the structure it disappeared into ultimate blackness. There was a curving corridor, heading downward in a wide spiral. He could see a dozen yards into it...then darkness obliterated his vision.

Templin shrugged and grinned tightly to himself. It looked so very much like a giant rat-trap. Foolish, to go into unknown danger on the chance that Ellen was there—

but it was the foolish sort of risk he had always been willing to take.

He snapped on his helmet lamp and stepped boldly in.

Down he went, and down. The corridor was roughly circular in section, slightly flattened underfoot and ornamented with ancient carvings. Templin flashed his light on them curiously as he passed. They were a repetition of the weirdly yearning figures he had seen on the columns outside—lean, tenuous manlike things, arms stretched to the sky. Curious, how like they were to human beings, Templin thought. Except for the leanness of them, and the outsize eyes on the pear-shaped head, they could almost have been men.

Templin grimaced at them and went on.

He had walked about a mile in the broad, downward spiral when he saw lights ahead.

Instinctively he snapped off his helmet lamp, stood motionless in the darkness, waiting to see if he had been noticed. But the lights, whatever they were, did not move; he waited for long minutes, and nothing came toward him. Obviously he had not been seen.

Templin cautiously moved up toward them, watching carefully. They were too bright for helmet lamps, he thought; and too still. But what other lights could be down here in this airless cavern under the Moon? He crept up behind a rock overhang and peered out.

"Good Lord!" Stunned, Templin spoke aloud, and the words echoed inside his helmet. For now he could see clearly—and what he saw was unbelievable.

There were figures moving before the lights. A stocky figure of a man in a pressure suit that Templin knew to be Olcott, and others. And the other figures were—not human!

TEMPLIN stepped out in the open to see more clearly. Abruptly some atavistic sense made the hair on his neck prickle with sudden warning of danger—but it came too late. Templin whirled around, suddenly conscious of his peril. Figures were behind him, menacing figures that he could not recognize in the darkness, closing in on him. He grabbed instinctively for his space knife, but before he had it clear of its scabbard they were on him, bowling him over with the force and speed of their silent attack. He fell heavily, with them on top of him.

He struggled, writhing frantically, but there were too many of them. They held him down; he felt hands running over him, plucking his space knife from its scabbard. Then he felt himself being picked up by a dozen hands and carried face down toward the lights.

Templin made his mind relax and consider, fighting to overcome his rage at being taken so by surprise. He thought desperately of ruses for escape...

Then anger was driven out of his mind. He heard a thin, shrill whistle of escaping air within his helmet. It meant only one thing...his suit had been pierced in the struggle, and his precious air was leaking into the void outside.

He made a supreme, convulsive effort and managed to free one arm, but it was recaptured immediately and he was helpless. Templin groaned internally. He was a dead man, he knew—dead as surely as though the heart had been cut from his body. For his suit was leaking air and there was no way to stop it, no nearby pressure-dome into which to flee, nothing to do but die.

Templin resigned himself for death; he relaxed, allowing his captors to carry him along at a swift, jogging trot. His mind was strangely calm, now that death was so near. For anxiety and fright come only from uncertainty...and there was no more uncertainty...in Templin's mind.

He felt his captors drop him ungently on a rock floor. They were close to the lights now, he realized...

The hiss of air in his ears was gone. And he was still alive. Templin dazedly comprehended a miracle, for the air in his helmet and suit had leaked out until, somehow, it had established a balance. And that meant—

"Air!" He said it aloud, and the word was a prayer of thanksgiving. It was no less than a miracle that there should be air here, under the surface of the Moon—a miracle for which Templin was deeply and personally grateful.

Someone laughed above him. He scrambled to his feet uncertainly, looking up. It was Olcott, pressure-suited but holding his helmet in his hand, laughing at him.

Olcott nodded in grim humor. "Yes," he said, his voice coming thinly to Templin through his own helmet, "it's air all right. But it won't matter to you, because you aren't going to live to enjoy it. My friends here will take care of that!"

Olcott jerked a thumb toward the lights. Templin followed with his eyes.

The lights were crude, old-fashioned electrics, grouped in front of a pit that descended into the floor of the cavern. And beyond the lights, standing in a stoic, silent group, were a dozen lean figures, big-eyed, bigheaded, wearing brief loincloths of some mineral material that glistened in the illumination.

Templin stared. For they were not human, those figures. They were the lean, questing figures that were carved in the ancient Lunarian stone.

TEMPLIN FORCED himself to turn to Olcott. He glanced at those who had captured him, half-expecting that they would be more of the ancient, supposedly extinct Lunarians. But again he was surprised, for the half-dozen men behind him were as human as himself though pale and curiously flabby looking. They wore shredded rags of cloth that seemed to Templin to be the remnants of a military uniform that had disappeared from the face of the Earth years before.

Groping for understanding, Templin turned back to Olcott. Then his mind cleared. There was one question to which he had to know the answer.

"Where's Ellen Bishop?" he demanded.

Olcott raised his heavy brows. "I was about to ask you that," he said. "Don't try to deceive me, Templin. Is she hiding?"

Templin shrugged without replying.

Olcott waved. "It doesn't matter. She can't get away. My patrols will pick her up—the Loonies are very good at that."

Templin looked at the dark man's eyes. It was impossible to read his expression, but Templin decided that he was telling the truth. There was no reason, after all, for him to lie.

Templin said shortly, "I don't know where she is." He pointed to the silent, watching figures beyond the lights. "What are they?"

Olcott chuckled richly. "They're the inhabitants, Templin. The original Lunarians. There aren't very many of them left—a thousand or so—but they're all mine."

Templin shook his head. Hard to believe, that the ancient race had survived for so long underground—yet he could not doubt it, when his eyes provided him with evidence. He said, "What do you mean, they're all yours?"

"They work for me," said Olcott easily. He gestured sharply, and the scarecrow-like figures bowed and began to descend into the pit, by a narrow spiral ramp around its sides. "They're rather useful, in fact. As you should know, considering how much they've helped me at Hyginus Cleft."

"Sabotage—you mean—these things were—"

Olcott nodded, almost purring in satisfaction. "Yes. The—accidents—to your equipment, the damage to your generators and a good many other things, were taken care of for me by the Loonies. For instance, it was one of them who located your plutonium pile for me."

Templin scowled. "Wearing one of my miners' pressure-suits, wasn't he? I begin to see." He looked at the group of pallid humans who had captured him. "They Loonies too?" he demanded.

Olcott shook his head. "Only by adoption," he said. "You see, they had the misfortune to be on the wrong side in the Three-Day War. In fact, they were some of the men who were operating the rocket projectors that were so annoying to the United Nations. And when your—*our*—compatriots began atom-blasting the rocket-launching sites, a few of them found their way down here." Olcott gazed at them benevolently. "They are very useful to me, too. They control the Loonies, you see—I think they must have been rather cruel to the Loonies when they first came, because the Loonies are frightened to death of them now. And I control *them.*"

Templin stiffened. "Rocket projectors," he repeated. "You mean these are the men who bombed Detroit?"

Olcott waved. "Perhaps," he said. "I don't know which targets they chose. This may have been the crew that blasted Paris—or Memphis—or Stalingrad."

Templin looked at them for a long moment. "I'll remember," he said softly. "My family— Never mind. What are you going to do with me?"

"I am very likely to kill you, Templin. Unless I turn you over to the Loonies for sport."

Templin nodded. "I see," he said. "Well, I—thought as much."

Olcott looked at him curiously. Then he issued a quick order to the pale, silent men behind him. It was not in English.

To Templin he said, "You shouldn't have gotten in my way. I need the uranium that your company owns; I plan to get it."

"Why?"

Olcott pursed his lips. "I think," he said, "that we will start the rocket projectors again. Only this time, there will be no slip-ups. As a high-ranking officer in the Security Patrol, I will make sure that we are not interfered with."

The pale men gripped Templin, carried him to the edge of the pit into which the Loonies had disappeared. Olcott said, "Goodbye, Templin. I'm turning you over to the Loonies. What they will do to you I don't know, but it will not be pleasant. They hate human beings." He smirked, and added, "With good reason."

He nodded to the men; they picked Templin up easily, dropped him into the pit.

It was not very deep. Templin dropped lightly perhaps twenty feet, landed easily and straightened to face whatever was coming.

He was surrounded by the tall, tenuous Lunarians, a dozen of them staring at him with their huge, cryptic eyes. Silently they gestured to him to move down a shaft in the rock. Templin shrugged and complied.

He was in a rabbit warren of tunnels, branching and forking out every few yards. Inside of a handful of minutes Templin was thoroughly confused.

They came to a vaulted dome in the rock. Still silent, the Lunarians gestured to Templin to enter. He did.

Someone came running toward him, crying, "Temp! Thank Heaven you're safe!"

Pressure suit off, dark hair flying as she ran to him, was Ellen.

CHAPTER SEVEN

TEMPLIN HELD her to him tightly for a long moment. When finally she stepped back he saw that her eyes were damp. She said, "Oh, Temp, I thought you were gone this time for sure! The Loonies told me that Olcott had captured you—I was so worried!"

Templin stared. "*Told* you? You mean these things can talk?"

"Well, no, not exactly. But they told me, all the same. It's mental telepathy, I suppose, Temp, or something very much like it. Oh, they can't read minds—unless you try to convey a thought—but they can project their own thoughts to another person. It sounds just like someone talking...but you don't hear it with your ears."

Templin nodded. "I begin to understand things," he said. "That miner at Hyginus—I thought I talked to him, and yet my radio was broken, so I couldn't have. And then, he abandoned his suit. Can the Loonies get along on the surface without pressure suits?"

Ellen looked uncertain. "I—I don't know. But—I think perhaps they can. They said something about Olcott forcing them to do it. Olcott has them under control, Temp. He's using them to get the uranium mines away from us—and the Loonies think he wants the uranium to make bombs!"

"I have heard about that," Templin said, "From Olcott. Which reminds me—how did you get down here without his knowing about it?"

Ellen said, "I was outside that Coliseum-looking place, up on the surface, and suddenly somebody grabbed me from behind. I was frightened half to death; he carried me down and through a bunch of tunnels to here. And then—why, this voice began talking to me, and it was one of the Loonies. He said—he said he wanted me to help him get rid of Olcott!"

Templin asked, "Why can't they get rid of him themselves? There are a couple thousand Loonies—and Olcott can't have more than fifteen or twenty men down here."

Ellen sighed. "That's the horrible thing, Temp. You see, these men haven't a thing to lose. When they came down here, they brought part of the warhead of an atom-rocket along. And they've got it assembled in one of the caverns, not far from here—right in the middle of a terrific big lode of uranium ore! Can you imagine what would happen if it went off, Temp? All that uranium would explode—the whole Moon would become a bomb. And that's what they're threatening to do if the Loonies try to fight them."

Templin whistled. He looked around the room they were in reflectively. It was a high-ceilinged, circular affair, cut out of the mother-rock, sparsely furnished with pallets and benches. Loonie living quarters, he thought.

He looked back at the hovering Lunarians, staring blankly at them from the entrance to the chamber. "How do you work this telepathy affair?" he demanded.

"Walk up to them and start talking. The effort of phrasing words is enough to convey the thought to them—as nearly as I can figure it out."

Templin nodded, looked at them again and walked slowly over. The bulbous heads with the giant eyes confronted him blankly. He said uncertainly, "Hello?"

A SENSATION of mirth reached him, as though someone had laughed silently beside his ear. A voice spoke, and he recognized its kinship to that of the "miner" he had stopped at Hyginus. It had the same curious strangeness, the thing that was not an accent but something more basic. It said, "Hello, Steve Templin. We have spared your life. Now tell us what we are to do with you."

"Why, I thought—" Steve stumbled. "That is, you're having trouble with these Earthmen, aren't you?"

"For sixteen of your years." There was anger in the thought. "We have not come to like Earthmen, Templin."

Templin said uncomfortably, "These Earthmen I don't like myself. Shall we make an alliance, then?"

The thought was direct and sincere. "It was for that that we spared your lives."

Templin nodded. "Good." Abruptly his whole bearing changed. He snapped, "Then help us get out of here! Get us back to Hadley Dome or Hyginus. We'll get help—and come back here and wipe them out!"

Regretfully, the Lunarian's thought came. "That, Templin, is impossible. Our people can go out into the vacuum unprotected, for short periods, but you cannot. Have you forgotten that your suit will no longer hold air?"

Templin winced. But he said, "Ellen's will. Let her go for help."

Wearily the thought came. "Again, no. For if you brought men here to help you, the Earthmen who enslave us could not be taken by surprise. And if only one of them should live for just a few moments after the first attack...it would be the death of us all. They have hollowed out a chamber in the midst of a deposit of the metal of fire. They have said that if we act against them they will set off a chain reaction—and, in this, I know that they do not lie."

The Lunarian hesitated. Almost apologetically he went on, "It was from the metal of fire that the greatness of our race was destroyed many thousands of years ago, Templin. Once we lived on the surface, and had atomic power; because we used it wrongly we ravished the surface of our planet and destroyed nearly all of our people. Now—there are so few of us left, Templin, and we must not see it happen again."

Templin spread his hands. "All right," he said shortly. "What you say is true. But what do you suggest we do?"

The thought was sympathetic. "There is only one chance," it said. "If someone could enter the chamber of the bomb— My own people cannot approach, for it is not allowed. But you are an Earthman; perhaps you could reach it. And if you could destroy the men who are in there—the others we can account for."

Templin gave it only a second's thought. He nodded reflectively. "It's the only chance," he agreed. "Well—lead the way. I'll try it."

THE LUNARIAN peeped out into a corridor, then turned back to Templin. He said in his soundless speech, "The entrance to the room of power is to your right. What you will find there I do not know, for none of us have ever been inside."

Templin shrugged. "All right," he said. And to Ellen Bishop, "This is it; if I shouldn't see you again—it's been worthwhile, Ellen."

The girl bit her lip. Impulsively she flung her arms around him, hugged him tight for a second. Then she stepped back and let him go.

Templin stepped out into the corridor. No one was in sight. He patted the bulge of Ellen's rocket pistol where it was concealed under his clothing—he had taken off his pressure suit, torn the stout fabric of his tunic to match the ragged uniforms he had seen on the pale men—and turned down the traveled path to his right.

Thirty yards along, he came to a metal door.

A man was standing there, looking dreamily at the rock wall of the corridor. He looked incuriously at Templin but made no move to stop him. As Templin passed, the man said something rapid and casual to him in the language of the nation that had waged the Three-Day War.

That was the first hurdle. It didn't sound like a challenge, Templin thought, wishing vainly that he had learned that language at some time in his life. Apparently the fugitives had not considered the possibility of an inimical human being penetrating to this place.

Templin replied with a non-committal grunt and walked on. The skin between his shoulder blades crawled, expecting the blast of a rocket-shell from the guard. But it did not come; the thing had worked.

Templin found that he was in a room where half a dozen men sat around, a couple of them playing cards with what looked like a homemade deck, others lying on pallets that had obviously been commandeered from the Loonies.

Along one wall was an involved mechanical affair—a metal tube with bulges along its fifteen-foot length, and a man standing by a push-button monitor control at one end of it. That was his target, Templin knew. Built like an atom bomb, it would have tiny fragments of uranium-235 or plutonium in it, ready to be hurled together to form a giant, self-detonating mass of atomic explosive at the touch of that button. And once the pieces had come together, nothing under the sun could prevent the blast.

The men were looking up at him, Templin saw. It was time to make his play. The thing was too much like shooting sitting ducks, he thought distastefully—yet he dared not warn them, give them a chance to fight back. Too much was at stake.

He gazed stolidly at the men who were looking at him, and his hand crept to where Ellen's rocket pistol was concealed inside his tunic.

"Templin!"

The shout was like a pistol-crack in his ears. Templin spun round frantically. And in the door stood Olcott, surprise and rage stamped on his face.

TEMPLIN whirled into action. The men in the room, abruptly conscious that something was wrong, were reaching for weapons. Templin made his decision and passed them up for the first shot—blasted, instead, the man at the atomic warhead control, most deadly to his plans. He saw the man's body disappear in incandescent red mist as the rocket shell hit, then fired at a clump of three who had weapons drawn, fired again and again. Surprise was with him, and he got each of them with his potent shells. Yet—the odds were too much against him. As he downed the last pale-skinned underground man, Olcott was on him!

Templin reeled with the fury of his attack, grunted as Olcott landed vicious stabbing blows on his unprotected body. He lost control of the rocket-pistol in his hand, saw it spin away across the room as Olcott thudded against him with his steel-gauntleted hand. Templin dropped to the floor under the pressure-suited body, rolled and brought his knees up in a savage kick. The chunky man grunted but lashed out and a steel fist caught Templin at the base of the jaw. For a second the chamber reeled around him. Another like that, he knew, and he was done.

Olcott came down on him like a metal and fabric colossus. The gauntleted hands reached for Templin's throat and found it, circled it and squeezed. Templin, battered and gasping in the thin air, found even that cut off under the remorseless pressure from the other's hands. He struggled with every trick he knew to break the man's grip.

Blindly his hands reached out, closed on something, heaved back. There was a sudden yielding, and Templin felt air reach his lungs once more. But it came too late.

Darkness overcame him…

SOMEONE WAS bending over him. Templin surged upward as soon as he opened his eyes. The figure leaped away and emitted a slight shriek. "Temp!" a voice said reprovingly.

Templin's eyes swam into focus again…it was Ellen.

He was in bed, in a huge room with filtered sunlight coming in through a giant window. He was on the surface—by the look of it, back at Hadley Dome.

His head throbbed. He touched it inquiringly, and his finger encountered gauze bandage. He stared at the girl.

"We won," she said simply. "The Loonies and I came in as soon as we could—soon as we heard the shooting. You did a terrific job, Temp. The only live ones in the room were you and Olcott. And, just as we came in— Olcott died."

"Died? Died how?"

"You broke his neck, Temp. He was strangling you, and you were fighting back, and you caught him under the chin and pushed. The metal collar of his pressure suit snapped his spine. And then, since you had a skull that's broken in three places, the surgeon says, you went off to sleep yourself."

Templin shook his head incredulously. "And the Loonies?"

"They're free. And very grateful to you, too. They— they massacred all the other Earthmen, down under there. They'd been waiting for the chance for years, you see. And—well, you've been unconscious for two days, and I've been busy. Things are under control now. The mine is back in operation—Culver's outside, waiting to see you—and you're free, too, Temp. You can go back to the Inner Planets whenever you like."

Templin repeated, "The Inner Planets." He looked at her and grinned. "It will be like a vacation," he said. "By the way, how about my bonus?"

"Bonus?" Ellen looked somewhat puzzled. Then she laughed—but a little strainedly, Templin decided. "Oh, you mean the backing that I promised you from Terralune? Well…it's yours, Temp. Ships, and money, and everything you need. Only—" She hesitated. "That is, I had an idea—"

He interrupted, "That's not what I mean," he objected. "My bonus was personnel. You promised me I could have help to settle Venus, if I took care of this mining affair for you. In fact, you said I could take my pick of anybody on the Terralune payroll."

Ellen's face clouded up. "Yes," she said. "But, Temp—"

"Don't argue," he commanded. "A promise is a promise. And—well, you're on the payroll, Ellen. My advice to you is, start packing. We leave for Venus in the morning!"

THE END

If you've enjoyed this book, you will not want to miss these terrific titles…

ARMCHAIR SCI-FI & HORROR DOUBLE NOVELS, $12.95 each

D-1   **THE GALAXY RAIDERS** by William P. McGivern
            SPACE STATION #1 by Frank Belknap Long

D-2   **THE PROGRAMMED PEOPLE** by Jack Sharkey
            SLAVES OF THE CRYSTAL BRAIN by William Carter Sawtelle

D-3   **YOU'RE ALL ALONE** by Fritz Leiber
            THE LIQUID MAN by Bernard C. Gilford

D-4   **CITADEL OF THE STAR LORDS** by Edmond Hamilton
            VOYAGE TO ETERNITY by Milton Lesser

D-5   **IRON MEN OF VENUS** by Don Wilcox
            THE MAN WITH ABSOLUTE MOTION by Noel Loomis

D-6   **WHO SOWS THE WIND…** by Rog Phillips
            THE PUZZLE PLANET by Robert A. W. Lowndes

D-7   **PLANET OF DREAD** by Murray Leinster
            TWICE UPON A TIME by Charles L. Fontenay

D-8   **THE TERROR OUT OF SPACE** by Dwight V. Swain
            QUEST OF THE GOLDEN APE by Paul W. Fairman & Milton Lesser

D-9   **SECRET OF MARRACOTT DEEP** by Henry Slesar
            PAWN OF THE BLACK FLEET by Mark Clifton.

D-10   **BEYOND THE RINGS OF SATURN** by Robert Moore Williams
            A MAN OBSESSED by Alan E. Nourse

ARMCHAIR SCIENCE FICTION CLASSICS, $12.95 each

C-1   **THE GREEN MAN**
            by Harold M. Sherman

C-2   **A TRACE OF MEMORY**
            By Keith Laumer

C-3   **INTO PLUTONIAN DEPTHS**
            by Stanton A. Coblentz

ARMCHAIR MASTERS OF SCIENCE FICTION SERIES, $16.95 each

M-1   **MASTERS OF SCIENCE FICTION, Vol. One**
            Bryce Walton—"Dark of the Moon" and other tales

M-2   **MASTERS OF SCIENCE FICTION, Vol. Two**
            Jerome Bixby—"One Way Street" and other tales

If you've enjoyed this book, you will not want to miss these terrific titles...

ARMCHAIR SCI-FI & HORROR DOUBLE NOVELS, $12.95 each

D-11   **PERIL OF THE STARMEN** by Kris Neville
           THE STRANGE INVASION by Murray Leinster

D-12   **THE STAR LORD** by Boyd Ellanby
           CAPTIVES OF THE FLAME by Samuel R. Delany

D-13   **MEN OF THE MORNING STAR** by Edmond Hamilton
           PLANET FOR PLUNDER by Hal Clement and Sam Merwin, Jr.

D-14   **ICE CITY OF THE GORGON** by Chester S. Geier and Richard Shaver
           WHEN THE WORLD TOTTERED by Lester del Rey

D-15   **WORLDS WITHOUT END** by Clifford D. Simak
           THE LAVENDER VINE OF DEATH by Don Wilcox

D-16   **SHADOW ON THE MOON** by Joe Gibson
           ARMAGEDDON EARTH by Geoff St. Reynard

D-17   **THE GIRL WHO LOVED DEATH** by Paul W. Fairman
           SLAVE PLANET by Laurence M. Janifer

D-18   **SECOND CHANCE** by J. F. Bone
           MISSION TO A DISTANT STAR by Frank Belknap Long

D-19   **THE SYNDIC** by C. M. Kornbluth
           FLIGHT TO FOREVER by Poul Anderson

D-20   **SOMEWHERE I'LL FIND YOU** by Milton Lesser
           THE TIME ARMADA by Fox B. Holden

ARMCHAIR SCIENCE FICTION CLASSICS, $12.95 each

C-4   **CORPUS EARTHLING**
        by Louis Charbonneau

C-5   **THE TIME DISSOLVER**
        by Jerry Sohl

C-6   **WEST OF THE SUN**
        by Edgar Pangborn

ARMCHAIR SCI-FI & HORROR GEMS SERIES, $12.95 each

G-1   **SCIENCE FICTION GEMS, Vol. One**
        Isaac Asimov and others

G-2   **HORROR GEMS, Vol. One**
        Carl Jacobi and others

If you've enjoyed this book, you will not want to miss these terrific titles…

ARMCHAIR SCI-FI & HORROR DOUBLE NOVELS, $12.95 each

D-21 **EMPIRE OF EVIL** by Robert Arnette
THE SIGN OF THE TIGER by Alan E. Nourse & J. A. Meyer

D-22 **OPERATION SQUARE PEG** by Frank Belknap Long
ENCHANTRESS OF VENUS by Leigh Brackett

D-23 **THE LIFE WATCH** by Lester del Rey
CREATURES OF THE ABYSS by Murray Leinster

D-24 **LEGION OF LAZARUS** by Edmond Hamilton
STAR HUNTER by Andre Norton

D-25 **EMPIRE OF WOMEN** by John Fletcher
ONE OF OUR CITIES IS MISSING by Irving Cox

D-26 **THE WRONG SIDE OF PARADISE** by Raymond F. Jones
THE INVOLUNTARY IMMORTALS by Rog Phillips

D-27 **EARTH QUARTER** by Damon Knight
ENVOY TO NEW WORLDS by Keith Laumer

D-28 **SLAVES TO THE METAL HORDE** by Milton Lesser
HUNTERS OUT OF TIME by Joseph E. Kelleam

D-29 **RX JUPITER SAVE US** by Ward Moore
BEWARE THE USURPERS by Geoff St. Reynard

D-30 **SECRET OF THE SERPENT** by Don Wilcox
CRUSADE ACROSS THE VOID by Dwight V. Swain

ARMCHAIR SCIENCE FICTION CLASSICS, $12.95 each

C-7 **THE SHAVER MYSTERY, Book One**
by Richard S. Shaver

C-8 **THE SHAVER MYSTERY, Book Two**
by Richard S. Shaver

C-9 **MURDER IN SPACE**
by David V. Reed

ARMCHAIR MASTERS OF SCIENCE FICTION SERIES, $16.95 each

M-3 **MASTERS OF SCIENCE FICTION, Vol. Three**
Robert Sheckley, "The Perfect Woman" and other tales

M-4 **MASTERS OF SCIENCE FICTION, Vol. Four**
Mack Reynolds, Part One, "Stowaway" and other tales

If you've enjoyed this book, you will not want to miss these terrific titles…

ARMCHAIR SCI-FI & HORROR DOUBLE NOVELS, $12.95 each

D-31 **A HOAX IN TIME** by Keith Laumer
INSIDE EARTH by Poul Anderson

D-32 **TERROR STATION** by Dwight V. Swain
THE WEAPON FROM ETERNITY by Dwight V. Swain

D-33 **THE SHIP FROM INFINITY** by Edmond Hamilton
TAKEOFF by C. M. Kornbluth

D-34 **THE METAL DOOM** by David H. Keller
TWELVE TIMES ZERO by Howard Browne

D-35 **HUNTERS OUT OF SPACE** by Joseph Kelleam
INVASION FROM THE DEEP by Paul W. Fairman,

D-36 **THE BEES OF DEATH** by Robert Moore Williams
A PLAGUE OF PYTHONS by Frederik Pohl

D-37 **THE LORDS OF QUARMALL** by Fritz Leiber and Harry Fischer
BEACON TO ELSEWHERE by James H. Schmitz

D-38 **BEYOND PLUTO** by John S. Campbell
ARTERY OF FIRE by Thomas N. Scortia

D-39 **SPECIAL DELIVERY** by Kris Neville
NO TIME FOR TOFFEE by Charles F. Meyers

D-40 **JUNGLE IN THE SKY** by Milton Lesser
RECALLED TO LIFE by Robert Silverberg

ARMCHAIR SCIENCE FICTION CLASSICS, $12.95 each

C-10 **MARS IS MY DESTINATION**
by Frank Belknap Long

C-11 **SPACE PLAGUE**
by George O. Smith

C-12 **SO SHALL YE REAP**
by Rog Phillips

ARMCHAIR SCI-FI & HORROR GEMS SERIES, $12.95 each

G-3 **SCIENCE FICTION GEMS, Vol. Two**
James Blish and others

G-4 **HORROR GEMS, Vol. Two**
Joseph Payne Brennan and others

If you've enjoyed this book, you will not want to miss these terrific titles...

ARMCHAIR SCI-FI & HORROR DOUBLE NOVELS, $12.95 each

D-81   **THE LAST PLEA** by Robert Bloch
THE STATUS CIVILIZATION by Robert Sheckley

D-82   **WOMAN FROM ANOTHER PLANET** by Frank Belknap Long
HOMECALLING by Judith Merril

D-83   **WHEN TWO WORLDS MEET** by Robert Moore Williams
THE MAN WHO HAD NO BRAINS by Jeff Sutton

D-84   **THE SPECTRE OF SUICIDE SWAMP** by E. K. Jarvis
IT'S MAGIC, YOU DOPE! by Jack Sharkey

D-85   **THE STARSHIP FROM SIRIUS** by Rog Phillips
FINAL WEAPON by Everett Cole

D-86   **TREASURE ON THUNDER MOON** by Edmond Hamilton
TRAIL OF THE ASTROGAR by Henry Haase

D-87   **THE VENUS ENIGMA** by Joe Gibson
THE WOMAN IN SKIN 13 by Paul W. Fairman

D-88   **THE MAD ROBOT** by William P. McGivern
THE RUNNING MAN by J. Holly Hunter

D-89   **VENGEANCE OF KYVOR** by Randall Garrett
AT THE EARTH'S CORE by Edgar Rice Burroughs

D-90   **DWELLERS OF THE DEEP** by Don Wilcox
NIGHT OF THE LONG KNIVES by Fritz Leiber

ARMCHAIR SCIENCE FICTION CLASSICS, $12.95 each

C-28   **THE MAN FROM TOMORROW**
by Stanton A. Coblentz

C-29   **THE GREEN MAN OF GRAYPEC**
by Festus Pragnell

C-30   **THE SHAVER MYSTERY, Book Four**
by Richard S. Shaver

ARMCHAIR MASTERS OF SCIENCE FICTION SERIES, $16.95 each

MS-7   **MASTERS OF SCIENCE FICTION AND FANTASY, Vol. Seven**
Lester del Rey, "The Band Played On" and other tales

MS-8   **MASTERS OF SCIENCE FICTION, Vol. Eight**
Milton Lesser, "'A' as in Android" and other tales

If you've enjoyed this book, you will not want to miss these terrific titles…

ARMCHAIR SCI-FI & HORROR DOUBLE NOVELS, $12.95 each

D-91 **THE TIME TRAP** by Henry Kuttner
THE LUNAR LICHEN by Hal Clement

D-92 **SARGASSO OF LOST STARSHIPS** by Poul Anderson
THE ICE QUEEN by Don Wilcox

D-93 **THE PRINCE OF SPACE** by Jack Williamson
POWER by Harl Vincent

D-94 **PLANET OF NO RETURN** by Howard Browne
THE ANNIHILATOR COMES by Ed Earl Repp

D-95 **THE SINISTER INVASION** by Edmond Hamilton
OPERATION TERROR by Murray Leinster

D-96 **TRANSIENT** by Ward Moore
THE WORLD-MOVER by George O. Smith

D-97 **FORTY DAYS HAS SEPTEMBER** by Milton Lesser
THE DEVIL'S PLANET by David Wright O'Brien

D-98 **THE CYBERENE** by Rog Phillips
BADGE OF INFAMY by Lester del Rey

D-99 **THE JUSTICE OF MARTIN BRAND** by Raymond A. Palmer
BRING BACK MY BRAIN by Dwight V. Swain

D-100 **WIDE-OPEN PLANET** by L. Sprague de Camp
AND THEN THE TOWN TOOK OFF by Richard Wilson

ARMCHAIR SCIENCE FICTION CLASSICS, $12.95 each

C-31 **THE GOLDEN GUARDSMEN**
by S. J. Byrne

C-32 **ONE AGAINST THE MOON**
by Donald A. Wollheim

C-33 **HIDDEN CITY**
by Chester S. Geier

ARMCHAIR SCI-FI & HORROR GEMS SERIES, $12.95 each

G-9 **SCIENCE FICTION GEMS, Vol. Five**
Clifford D. Simak and others

G-10 **HORROR GEMS, Vol. Five**
E. Hoffman Price and others

If you've enjoyed this book, you will not want to miss these terrific titles…

ARMCHAIR SCI-FI & HORROR DOUBLE NOVELS, $12.95 each

D-101 **THE CONQUEST OF THE PLANETS** by John W. Campbell
THE MAN WHO ANNEXED THE MOON by Bob Olsen

D-102 **WEAPON FROM THE STARS** by Rog Phillips
THE EARTH WAR by Mack Reynolds

D-103 **THE ALIEN INTELLIGENCE** by Jack Williamson
INTO THE FOURTH DIMENSION by Ray Cummings

D-104 **THE CRYSTAL PLANETOIDS** by Stanton A. Coblentz
SURVIVORS FROM 9,000 B. C. by Robert Moore Williams

D-105 **THE TIME PROJECTOR** by David H. Keller, M.D. and David Lasser
STRANGE COMPULSION by Philip Jose Farmer

D-106 **WHOM THE GODS WOULD SLAY** by Paul W. Fairman
MEN IN THE WALLS by William Tenn

D-107 **LOCKED WORLDS** by Edmond Hamilton
THE LAND THAT TIME FORGOT by Edgar Rice Burroughs

D-108 **STAY OUT OF SPACE** by Dwight V. Swain
REBELS OF THE RED PLANET by Charles L. Fontenay

D-109 **THE METAMORPHS** by S. J. Byrne
MICROCOSMIC BUCCANEERS by Harl Vincent

D-110 **YOU CAN'T ESCAPE FROM MARS** by E. K. Jarvis
THE MAN WITH FIVE LIVES by David V. Reed

ARMCHAIR SCIENCE FICTION CLASSICS, $12.95 each

C-34 **30 DAY WONDER**
by Richard Wilson

C-35 **G.O.G. 666**
by John Taine

C-36 **RALPH 124C 41+**
by Hugo Gernsback

ARMCHAIR SCI-FI & HORROR GEMS SERIES, $12.95 each

G-11 **SCIENCE FICTION GEMS, Vol. Six**
Edmond Hamilton and others

G-12 **HORROR GEMS, Vol. Six**
H. P. Lovecraft and others

If you've enjoyed this book, you will not want to miss these terrific titles…

ARMCHAIR SCI-FI & HORROR DOUBLE NOVELS, $12.95 each

D-111 **THE MOON ERA** by Jack Williamson
REVENGE OF THE ROBOTS by Howard Browne

D-112 **SON OF THE BLACK CHALICE** by Milton Lesser
SENTRY OF THE SKY by Evelyn E. Smith

D-113 **OUTPOST ON THE MOON** by Joslyn Maxwell
POTENTIAL ZERO by S. J. Byrne

D-114 **OUTPOST INFINITY** by Raymond F. Jones
THE WHITE INVADERS by Ray Cummings

D-115 **TIME TRAP** by Rog Phillips
THE COSMIC DESTROYER by Alexander Blade

D-116 **THE OTHER SIDE OF THE MOON** by Edmond Hamilton
SECRET INVASION by Walter Kubilius

D-117 **DANGER MOON** by Frederik Pohl
THE HIDDEN UNIVERSE by Ralph Milne Farley

D-118 **THE WAILING ASTEROID** by Murray Leinster
THE WORLD THAT COULDN'T BE by Clifford D. Simak

D-119 **THE WHISPERING GORILLA** by Don Wilcox
RETURN OF THE WHISPERING GORILLA by David V. Reed

D-120 **SPECIAL EFFECT** by J. F. Bone
WARLORD OF KOR by Terry Carr

ARMCHAIR SCIENCE FICTION CLASSICS, $12.95 each

C-37 **THE GREEN MAN RETURNS**
by Harold M. Sherman

C-38 **THE SHAVER MYSTERY, Book Five**
by Richard S, Shaver

C-39 **MARS CHILD**
by Cyril Judd

ARMCHAIR MASTERS OF SCIENCE FICTION SERIES, $16.95 each

MS-9 **MASTERS OF SCIENCE FICTION AND FANTASY, Vol. Nine**
Poul Anderson, "The Star Beast" and other tales

MS-10 **MASTERS OF SCIENCE FICTION, Vol. Ten**
Robert Moore Williams, "Time Tolls for Toro" and other tales

WERE THEY STILL ON EARTH, OR SOMEWHERE UNKNOWN?

Bob Cathcart was happy when his brother, Johnny, had landed a job with the gigantic Frain Corporation. Johnny had signed on and was shipped off to one of Malcolm Frain's secret industrial colonies. But that had been six months earlier, and that was the last time Bob Cathcart had seen or heard from his brother. So with his career as a chemical researcher going nowhere, Bob decided to take a job as a truck driver for the Frain Corporation, partially in hope of finding out what had happened to his missing brother.

Like his brother before him, he was also shipped out to one of Malcolm Frain's secret colonies. But after his arrival, it didn't take Bob Cathcart long to discover that the colony he had come to was like no place he had ever seen. In fact, he soon came to the grim realization that this colony might not even be located on Earth!

CAST OF CHARACTERS

BOB CATHCART
This truck driver had a chance to rebuild his career as a chemist by taking a mystery job with the world's biggest corporation.

DONNA FRAIN
She was the beautiful daughter of one of the world's richest men—tough as nails, but a soft spot in her heart, too.

DR. FREUNDLICH
His scientific research came to one startling conclusion—he and his fellow colonists were no longer on Earth!

PUTORIOUS TERRO
He was basically a street-smart thug with a lot of ambition; but ambitious thugs can be a dangerous thing.

MICKEY FOLEY
Reporters weren't allowed at the Frain industrial complex, which was exactly why this reporter applied for a position there.

MALCOLM FRAIN
He was perhaps the wealthiest, most powerful businessman on Earth—but did all that power instill any sense of patriotism?

THE HIDDEN UNIVERSE

By
RALPH MILNE FARLEY

ARMCHAIR FICTION & MUSIC
PO Box 4369, Medford, Oregon 97504

*For more information about Armchair Books and products, visit our
website at…*

www.armchairfiction.com

Or email us at…

armchairfiction@yahoo.com

CHAPTER ONE
Multimillionaire Man of Mystery

FRAIN City, New Jersey, center of the far-flung industrial empire of billionaire Malcolm Frain.

On all sides towered factory buildings, devoted to the manufacture of hundreds of products—massive machinery, household utensils, hairpins, locomotives, battleships, and cosmetics. Each factory bore the name of Frain, and from twin flagstaffs on every building fluttered the Stars and Stripes; and another flag: a red "F" in a white circle on a blue field. The streets were jammed with trucks, carting the Frain products to the Hudson River docks, there to be loaded on Frain Line steamers, which would carry them to the principal ports of the world.

Along one of these crowded thoroughfares walked two truck drivers in trim black uniforms and shiny puttees. One was stocky and swarthy; the other, tall and blond and sandy haired.

The dark one stared aloft at the towering factories. "They say Malcolm Frain is worth twenty billions— billions, Cathcart, not millions!" He spat vehemently, as though to show his contempt for all that wealth.

Cathcart grunted absently. There were lines of worry on his blond face, and his thoughts were far away from any consideration of Malcolm Frain's fabulous fortune.

His swarthy companion, nettled at his lack of response, snapped. "What's eating you, Cathcart?"

"It's this mysterious hocus-pocus that pervades the Frain

organization," Cathcart replied. "Here we are, Terro, on our way to Headquarters, and we haven't the slightest idea why they have sent for us. Maybe they're going to ship us off to one of the Frain colonies, without even asking if we wish to go. Where are these colonies, anyway? This secrecy is getting on my nerves."

"They don't keep any secrets from me," Terro taunted. "Perhaps they take you for a reporter—Frain won't let a newshawk set foot this side of the Hudson. I know why they sent for me. I'm going to be promoted and shipped to one of the colonies."

"Which one?"

Terro shrugged. "No use to ask that. They never tell—just ship a feller off. Maybe a banana plantation, or one of his African rubber forests. Maybe his Arabian oil fields. Not that I care; to hell with 'em, so long as I get what's coming to me."

"Yes, they never tell," said Cathcart, as though talking to himself. "And no¬ one ever writes back. I haven't heard once from my brother."

"Well, I should worry," Terro laughed irritatingly. "My new job will mean less work, more pay, and a change from wheeling these damn trucks day and night. And there should be a good chance for graft that far from Headquarters."

The two drivers reached a towering building of shiny black tile, chromium plate, and translucent glass blocks. Entering, they gave their names to a black¬-uniformed official at a desk just inside the door and were directed to a reception hall at the rear of the ground floor.

AS Cathcart and Terro started down the corridor, they had to step aside to make way for a jostling throng of about five hundred men, women, and children, laden with bundles, bags, and suitcases. These people were being herded out of the building by a score or so of black-uniformed guards. The men looked exalted and determined; the women, somewhat apprehensive; the children, happy and excited.

These folks were en route to one of the Frain colonies, the two truck drivers knew. Turning, Cathcart and Terro watched the colonists tramp out the front door to be loaded into busses and driven toward the docks, bound for no one knew whither. Cathcart pictured his brother departing like that, six months ago. In one of the pockets of Cathcart's black blouse was the last letter he had received from Johnny. He had read it so often he knew it by heart:

Dear Bob:

I've got my chance at last. Am being shipped to one of the Frain plantations. Africa, I believe, although the employment office is a bit indefinite about that.

But they did impress upon me that the mail-service between there and the States is irregular, and that the operations of the plantation are secret. So I was told to notify my family not to worry if they don't hear from me. You are my only family, so this is the notification.

Anyway, my new job is a promotion, and it means a big raise in pay; so congratulate me. I'll write again as soon as permitted.

Yours, John.

Fine for Johnny, winning a promotion in one of the most reputable and outstanding industrial organizations of America! Yet somehow the letter hadn't rung quite true, although Bob Cathcart at the time had been so engrossed in chemical experimentation that he had been only vaguely conscious of that fact.

Two months later the entire technical staff of the Chemical Foundation for which Cathcart worked had suddenly been laid off. After another month, unable to secure any work in his own line, and worried because he had not heard from Johnny again, Cathcart had secured a job with the Frain Truck Lines, Inc., not only because it was the only work available in the depths of a depression, but also in the hope that he might thereby get some clue as to what had become of his brother.

Cathcart had telephoned the Frain employment office several times to inquire about his brother, but always was put off with the vague reply, "He's well, and likes his new work. Write him, care of us, and we'll forward your letter." Cathcart had written repeatedly, but no reply had ever come.

With a sigh, Cathcart now turned and followed Terro down the hallway to the room that the doorman had indicated. It resembled the waiting room of a railroad station. About two hundred men—most of them in black uniforms, but some in business suits, and a few in overalls—sat on the benches, chatting in whispers or rustling newspapers, or shifting nervously in their seats.

As Cathcart and Terro sat down in a vacant space, Cathcart's attention fell on the headline of a New York tabloid newspaper lying besides him:

MULTIMILLIONAIRE MAN OF MYSTERY

Beneath this headline was a picture, evidently a composite, showing Malcolm Frain's head combined rather crudely with a black uniformed body. The caption was:

Is Malcolm Frain a philanthropist, or a financial wizard, or both, or neither? (Story, page 16).

Cathcart turned to page 16, and read:

How is Malcolm Frain able to hire one thousand unemployed a day, when all the other industrialists are laying men off? Even Frain's billions can't last forever, for unlike the Federal Government, he does not have unlimited credit—nor any Social Security funds that he can divert to finance a deficit.

His price-cuts are threatening the solvency of his competitors and they are keeping all the factories of his private city over in Jersey operating full time; yet no business can endure without profits, and profit seems impossible at the prices that Frain is charging.

Nevertheless Malcolm Frain is today doing more to relieve unemployment than all the Federal, State, and Municipal agencies combined!

What is Frain's secret? Why is he hiring all these men? What is he doing with them?

Certainly his factories, even running three shifts as they are, are not large enough to absorb all the men whom he is hiring. The New Jersey State Commissioner of Labor refuses to give out any information as to the growth of Frain's employment, but this was to be expected in view of Frain's strangle-hold on the politics of that state.

Perhaps Malcolm Frain is shipping these thousands of new employees to his rubber forests, his banana plantations, and his oil fields; but after the beating that his armed thugs gave our reporter yesterday (see picture), we are inclined to hazard the guess that there is something rotten about the whole performance, although we are not yet quite prepared to accuse him of being a second 'Bishop of Bingen.' "

Cathcart whistled. "That comes darn close to libel!" he exclaimed.

Terro reached for the newspaper. "Hmm! It's okay with me anything they say about the boss. He's making plenty of money out of our labor, without him turning a hand."

"He's giving both of us jobs at good pay in the depths of a depression," Cathcart reminded him.

Terro spat on the floor, and began spelling out the words of the newspaper¬ item. When he reached the end, he asked, "Who's this 'Bishop of Bingen' they're talking about?"

"Oh, a fellow years ago, who offered to put an end to poverty and unemployment. He herded all the paupers who answered his advertisement into a hall. Then he burned the hall down over their heads, thereby making good his promise."

Suddenly Terro sat erect, whistled softly, and nudged Cathcart. "I'll take a chance at being burned, if that's the torch." Terro nudged Cathcart again, and grimaced toward a slim girl in the black uniform of the Frain guards, who had just entered the waiting room and was mounting a platform at one end of the hall. On her black military cap was the word "Inspector."

CATHCART studied the girl appraisingly. Strange that such a young girl should occupy such a high position in the ranks of the Frain organization. Strange even that one of her sex should be in uniform at all.

As Cathcart stared, his curiosity changed to admiration. The cool calm assurance of the girl intrigued him. And yet for all her evident capability, she was not the mannish type. Not in the least. Not even boyish. Her features were pink-and-white and cameo-cut. Vagrant wisps of copper-gold hair strayed from beneath the rim of her military cap. Her lips, though firm, were delicately curved. Her figure, in spite of its alertness, was soft with feminine roundness.

Cathcart's keen gray eyes crinkled, and he nodded quietly to himself.

His thoughts were interrupted by the harsh voice of Terro, "Some baby, eh? The guy that gets her is going to have a soft job from then on. She's Frain's brat."

"So that's Donna Frain..." whispered Cathcart.

The girl herself now spoke in a clear cool voice, "Attention, please! You all know what you have been called here for—promotion to positions in one of the colonies. I am not at liberty to say which. Your pay will be at least twice what you are now getting. Those of you who are chosen for special work will receive even more. Your immediate family will accompany you. But you must sign up for five years."

Five years! Those words staggered Cathcart out of his rapt study of Donna Frain. Would the bare chance of being sent to the same colony as his brother be worth the risk of being sent to the wrong colony and getting stuck there for five years?

Donna Frain went on, "The mails are very uncertain, and the operations of my father's colonies are rather secret; so—"

Yet, Cathcart had learned as much from that well-remembered letter in his breast pocket. Again he mused upon his brother's fate. Had Johnny and his fellow colonists been put to death, as the legendary Bishop of Bingen had killed the paupers to cure their poverty? Was that to be his own fate too, if he followed in his brother's footsteps? He turned his attention back to the flaming-haired girl, just in time to hear her conclude her address with the scarcely veiled threat, "If you do not accept, we may have to replace you with other prospective colonists. Remember: jobs are scarce these days. But if you are prepared to accept, or wish further information, please wait here until your name is called; then report to whatever inspector is in charge of the room indicated."

Cathcart's eyes followed her trim uniformed figure as she walked briskly from the hall. Surely she would not be a party to any sinister trickery. What a girl! And yet how unattainable—the daughter of America's richest multimillionaire, and a high-ranking official in the organization in which Cathcart himself was a mere pawn.

Terro's rasping voice obtruded upon his reverie with, "Did it ever occur to you what a sweet racket a fellow would have if he could only get something on Malcolm Frain?" Terro's narrow-eyed swarthy face was thrust close to Cathcart.

Accumulated irritation burst from Cathcart. "Did it ever occur to you," he snapped, "what a sweet chance you'd have of getting kicked out of the service, if someone got something on you?"

Just then he heard his own name being read off: "Robert Cathcart. Room 2." He got up and headed for the designated doorway.

IN the cubicle to which Door No. 2 admitted him, Inspector Donna Frain sat at a desk. Her military cap was off, exposing in its full glory the aureole of her burnished copper-gold hair. Her perfect features showed even more perfect at close scrutiny. Her jade-green eyes were cool and inscrutable.

Cathcart grinned ingratiatingly. Snapping into action in front of the desk, he began, "Miss Frain—"

"Address me as 'Inspector'," she interrupted with

dignity, although not unkindly. "Surely you have been long enough in the service to know that."

"Yes, Inspector," Cathcart replied with assumed meekness, but there was an irrepressible twinkle in his gray eyes.

"That's better." Donna Frain softened somewhat. "Well, Cathcart, how would you like the position of assistant chemist in one of our colonies?"

"Very much, Inspector. I had expected just another trucking job." His gray eyes glowed at the thought of test tubes and Bunsen-burners again.

"You would have been chosen before," Donna Frain continued, "but we first had to check up and make certain that you had no newspaper connections. You know the rule against reporters?"

"Yes, Inspector."

"Well, our Secret Service has checked up on you and has found that you are not a newspaperman. Also that you are a bachelor with no immediate relatives in the region. You have received no mail, except technical chemical communications, since you have been with us. You have been a loyal and industrious member of the Frain organization. You can start for your new job this afternoon, if you wish."

"May I ask, Inspector, the nature of the chemical work that I'm to undertake?"

"I suppose you are leading up to an inquiry as to where you are to be sent?" Her pretty features hardened. "Employees of Malcolm Frain ask no questions; and, when they do, they receive no answers. And now I shall ask you a question. Why did you not apply to us for work as a chemical engineer in the first place?"

"Hasn't your vaunted Secret Service found out that for

you?" he countered, a bit maliciously.

"Cathcart!" she snapped. "Answer my question…"

He did some quick thinking and finally decided to risk the truth. "Well, Miss, I'll be frank with you. I wanted to get sent to one of your colonies, and it seemed to me that I'd have a better chance as a mere laborer. I'm trying to find my brother John, who disappeared to one of your colonies six months ago."

"Um! And it never occurred to you to come directly to Headquarters and ask about him?"

"I asked repeatedly, but was always given the same evasive answer. I wrote repeatedly to my brother, but never received a reply."

"Well, we'll find out right now." She pushed one of the red buttons of an inter-office switchbox on her desk, and lifted her telephone from its cradle.

"Hello! Records Department? Inspector Donna Frain speaking. Send the dossier of John Cathcart down to Cubicle 2 in the waiting room. Right away." She hung up, and turned to Bob Cathcart with just the trace of a smile on her perfect features. "I rather think that we can assign you to the same colony as your brother."

He grinned back at her, and said with feeling, "Thank you very much, Inspector. And now may I ask you a question? Do you ever visit this colony?"

"What's that to you?"

"A workingman is always interested in what sort of superiors he works for." Cathcart's manner was respectful and disarming.

"I thought you were interested in finding your brother."

"I am. But five years is a long time to sign up for, without additional inducements."

She colored slightly. "Cathcart!"

A knock. The door opened, and a messenger came in, deposited a large manila envelope on the desk, and withdrew. Donna Frain covered her embarrassment by fumbling in the envelope and studying its contents. Bob Cathcart continued to stand at attention; he knew when not to go too far.

"Yes," said Donna, returning the file to its container. "Your brother John, although formerly assigned to another of our colonies, is now at the one to which you are about to be sent. You will find him there at Town No. 13. Is that sufficient to you?"

"No," Cathcart replied in a quiet level voice. "You haven't yet answered my question. Shall I ever see you at that colony?" An amused smile hovered around the corners of his mouth.

Her own eyes fell. "I plan to visit that colony frequently," she said softly.

"Good!" Cathcart exulted. "Then I shall gladly enlist in your service."

CHAPTER TWO
Facilis Descensus Averni

DONNA Frain smiled up at him. "I think that we shall enjoy working together, Cathcart." Then, with a resumption of her crisp military manner, "Return to the Truck Lines barracks and pack at once. Report back here at four o'clock. Everything that you need for immediate use you had better carry, as it may be a month before your boxes will follow. We will notify your dispatcher of your transfer."

As Cathcart briskly saluted and strode from the cubicle, his pulses were racing. Undoubtedly because his quest for his brother was so nearly at an end, he told himself.

Terro was no longer seated on the bench outside in the waiting room. Cathcart grinned. This meant either that that pest had been called into some other cubicle than Donna Frain's, or that he had gotten cold feet about being shipped off to an unknown destination. Either alternative was satisfactory to Cathcart.

Humming to himself, Cathcart ran down the steps of the garish Administration Building, and strode with the stream of dock-bound trucks to the barracks behind the huge terminal garage of the Frain Truck and Bus Lines.

On the stroke of four he was back at the Administration Building with two suitcases, and was herded into a hall with several hundred men, women, and children, laden with bags and bundles. Terro was among them—too bad! An Inspector checked off the names of the group. Then they were all marched out of the building, loaded into busses, and driven to the docks.

The men and women in the bus with Cathcart were fidgety and uneasy. They conversed in nervous whispers. They stared out of the windows at the passing buildings as though loath to leave these familiar scenes. Even the children, sensing the moods of their parents, were wide-eyed and subdued.

Several of the women were hunched and sobbing. One of them, seated next to Cathcart, timidly inquired, "You— ¬you're in uniform—one of Mr. Frain's soldiers. You think it's all right, don't you? For us to go to the colonies, I mean."

Cathcart did his best to reassure her, but his words lacked conviction. After all, what did he himself know about their mysteriously concealed destination?

The busses drew up at a huge waterfront storehouse, a new one that had been in the process of construction when Cathcart had first come to work for the Frain Industries three months ago. Here, as the building had neared completion, Cathcart had brought truckload after truckload of fine silt from the laboratories of the Frain Chemical Foundation. As a chemist himself, he had wondered why and how all this dirt was being treated in the laboratories; but one learns in the service of Malcolm Frain not to ask questions.

At this building the five hundred colonists were now herded into a large vacant storeroom. Cathcart's insignia, a gold autowheel on each lapel, were removed, as were the insignia of such other colonists as wore the black uniform: cogwheels for the factory employees, wings and propeller for the airlines, etc. All baggage was thoroughly searched. White brassards bearing the letter "C" in black, were pinned onto the arms of all the colonists.

"Do we wear this until we reach the colony?" Cathcart asked, as the guard was pinning his on.

The guard stared at him intently, suspiciously. "Are you trying to be funny?" he asked. "How long a trip do you think it is?"

"Well, how long is it?" Cathcart asked.

"None of your business. If you know what's good for you, you won't get too nosey."

Cathcart shrugged his broad shoulders and subsided.

HE glanced around the storeroom at the cowering colonists and the bustling officious guards. It was a bare concrete room, with sprinkler heads and water pipes overhead.

Names were now read off a list, Putorius Terro's among them, and about a hundred of the colonists were herded with their baggage into a large elevator, the doors of which slid soundlessly shut behind them.

Cathcart and the rest of the colonists waited, alert and nervous. About three¬-quarters of an hour elapsed; then the elevator doors opened, and a second batch of colonists were herded in.

Girls wearing the conventional Frain uniform now went among the remaining colonists distributing coffee and sandwiches. Three-quarters of an hour later another hundred colonists entered the elevator, Cathcart looked at his wristwatch; the time was seven o'clock. Evening shadows were falling; the lights were turned on in the huge storeroom.

As he waited, Cathcart studied the storeroom in which he stood. He remembered it well, for it was to this very room that he had trucked his loads of silt; only then there had been no elevator, not even an opening for an elevator shaft either up or down where the elevator doors now indicated one to be. He studied his fellow colonists; the wait was getting on their nerves, men and women were pacing up and down, or nagging at each other, children were whining or snarling. Cathcart turned his thought to "Inspector" Donna Frain.

He was still daydreaming about the flaming-haired girl, when at eight-thirty it finally came his turn, as one of the last hundred. The elevator-cage into which they were led was lined with some smooth iridescent composition, without so much as a crack to give view of the shaft in which it hung. The doors slid shut, and then were wedged solidly in place by guards turning handwheels on the inside, as though the intention was to seal the elevator-car hermetically. Cathcart stared up at the top of the car, which was dotted with incandescent electric lights, interlaced with inert glass tubes.

He was vaguely attempting to puzzle out the purpose of these tubes when his thoughts were interrupted by a woman's scream from the far side of the car: "Let me out! Where are you taking us?" She began to hammer on the walls with her hands.

One of the guards standing nearby seized the woman firmly, but not unkindly, and tried to quiet her; but as a result she merely shrieked the louder. Her terror was contagious. Cathcart, sensing trouble, pushed his way toward her through the throng; but a husky man in overalls, evidently the woman's husband, reached the spot ahead of him and drove a ham-like fist to the guard's jaw. The guard went down.

INSTANTLY the whole elevator-car was in a turmoil.

Women, and even some of the men, clamoring: "Let me out! Let me out!"

One of the guards grabbed Cathcart's elbow. "Hey, you! You look sane. Help us quell this riot."

Clubs began to fly, cracking skulls. Cathcart flung a protective arm about an hysterical woman, drew her out of the melee, and shook her gently until her eyes lost their fixed stare and returned to normal. He slapped a man across the mouth, who was just about to scream.

The authoritative voice of the Corporal in charge of the guards sounded above the, din: "Quiet! Quiet, youse! There is no way to get out of this room until we reach the colony, so youse might just as well shut up."

"Colony!" "Are we already on the way?" Those who were still on their feet gasped, and then subsided into complete and sodden silence. In the lull, Cathcart noted that the lights on the ceiling had gone out, and that some of the glass tubes were now glowing white.

Twenty minutes later the doors on the opposite side of the elevator swung open upon a concrete storeroom, very much like that from which they had entered the elevator. The Corporal in charge handed over a packet of papers to another Corporal who stood waiting with his own squad outside.

"Had a riot," the first Corporal laconically reported. "Tried to avoid it, but I had to keep order."

"Okay," the other replied, unimpressed. "Hey there, you colonists. Cart out the wounded." Then, turning to one of his men, "Count 'em, and then send to the hospital for the necessary number of stretchers."

Cathcart helped carry out and lay on the hard cold concrete floor those who had been battered, about twenty in number. Cathcart's jaw was set, and his gray eyes were slits. Although he realized that the guards had used their clubs only as a last resort, and that otherwise the colonists would have done more harm to themselves and each other than the guards had done; yet this brutality, necessary though it was, stirred up in him an instinctive resentment.

The doors of the elevator closed behind him with a fatalistic finality.

"Come on, the rest of you," commanded the new Corporal, "and make it snappy!"

Through a wide high doorway they were led out onto a driveway in the open. An indescribable air of unreality pervaded the place. Far above their heads a solid unmoving unruffled bank of white clouds shed a shadowless radiance as bright as the full glare of sunlight.

Flush behind the concrete storehouse from which they had just come, there rose a sheer cliff of rough white stone, to merge with the clouds above. In front of them, and away to the left, stretched a level plain of rich farming land, with here and there a village or a wood in the distance.

Nothing so very unusual, except the flat unchanging sky and the steep cliff; and yet none of the colors of the landscape were quite right, and there was an eerie soughing sound of wind overhead.

Off to the right, and also abutting the cliff, was a chromium and black office building, reminiscent of Headquarters in Frain City, N. J., but smaller; and beyond it lay several substantial brick barracks, flanked by a sizeable small city.

According to Cathcart's wristwatch, it was now 9:00 p.m., but the clock on the office building said quarter past four! He set his own watch to the changed time.

THE Corporal marched them to the barracks, where the

single men and women were assigned to neat but rather bare rooms, and the families to suites. They were all instructed to stow their belongings and then report to the Administration Building in fifteen minutes, leaving the children behind. Nurses would take care of the children. There was no sign of the four installments of colonists who had preceded them.

At the Administration Building, they were herded into a lecture room. As soon as they were comfortably seated, an Inspector with white hair and a jolly, friendly face mounted the platform and addressed them.

"Welcome to Utopia," he began. "It is unfortunate that your entry into this new state of existence should have been marred by rioting, suppressed by what may seem to you to have been unnecessary severity. But order must be preserved in this colony, for your own good.

"You will find that life here among us is idyllic far beyond anything of which you have ever dreamed. Each adult individual will be permitted to pick out a city lot of land or a country tract. On this lot or tract he or she can build a home on easy terms. Homesteads can be exchanged, subject to just merely enough supervision to guarantee that no one gets cheated. Your land can never be taken away by lawsuits, your pay cannot be garnisheed, and there are no taxes. There is no relief, for here everyone has a job.

"Medical attention is free, and one's pay continues indefinitely during any bona fide disability or illness. Education for the children is free, and they can continue in grammar school, high school, or college, as far as their abilities entitle them. You will all spend tonight in the barracks. Tomorrow you will be shipped to the scene of your new jobs. Any question?"

"How about churches?" asked one of the women.

"Each of the towns has at least one church," the Inspector replied, "and your places of work have been selected with a view to your expressed religious preferences."

"Where are we?" asked Cathcart.

"I was just coming to that. You are no longer in the world. You are not even on another planet of the solar system. You are not even in the same universe as that in which you were this morning. The cage that brought you here and that you thought was a mere elevator, is a status-changing machine that has literally transported you into a new state of existence. Even time here has no relation to the time of the world from which you have come; for example, a person who left the world before you did, and who spent the same length of time getting here, may not yet have arrived." He then paused, as though for a dramatic effect.

Cathcart broke the awed silence by asking, "And conversely a person who has not yet left the Earth may already be here?"

He had merely been trying to relieve his tenseness by a little bit of humor, but to his horrified surprise the Inspector then replied, "That's exactly right. So you can see why our newspapers here carry no news of contemporary events of the world. Events there are not contemporary."

Cathcart's jaw dropped. Hooey? And yet the Inspector had spoken with evident sincerity. Cathcart sat erect and listened with fascinated intentness as the Inspector continued, "The universe to which you have been accustomed consists of specks of matter—¬stars and planets—floating in empty space. But this universe, where we now are, consists of holes in solid space."

"Sort of like a cheese," someone whispered behind Cathcart. One of the women colonists tittered nervously.

Meanwhile the Inspector was saying, "We are in one of these holes now. Other such holes have been discovered and colonized. This one is almost exactly thirty-nine and a half miles square, and its height has been estimated at about four miles. There are no seasons here. Every day is exactly twelve hours long, and so is every night. Rain falls only at night. A luminous glow takes the place of the sun. For convenience, we call thirty-two days a month, and twelve months a year. Any more questions?"

There were none. The audience was too dazed to ask any.

"You will now return to the barracks," the Inspector concluded. "Let me give you all a final caution. This entire world is governed by the will of Malcolm Frain, who is here known as 'the Boss.' You are no longer citizens of the United States of America. But, if you work faithfully and keep the peace, you will be more prosperous, better cared for, and happier than would have been possible in the old world, which you have now left behind you...forever..."

A STUNNED silence greeted this last announcement.

Then a woman shrieked despairingly, "Forever?"

And a man cried out, "We signed up for only five years!"

An ominous rumble began to swell through the crowd, but it petered out again. The colonists were so stunned by what had gone before, as to be numb to this final blow.

The Inspector's round face was sympathetic and his voice was soothing, as he continued. "Dear friends, when

you have been here with us for a little while, you will not
wish to return to the Earth. And you will appreciate the
wisdom of the Boss in not letting you return. For, if
stories were spread about this truly wonderful domain of
his, he would be mobbed by millions of people, demanding
to be sent here. This idyllic utopia is available only to
picked individuals like yourselves. Now return to your
lodgings."

As Cathcart filed out of the hall with the others, his
mind was in a daze. All this preposterous talk about a new
universe might be acceptable to the common run of these
colonists; but Cathcart was a scientifically trained man, a
chemist, and to him it was simply absurd!

Never in his life had he felt so cooped up, so utterly
alone. Even the fact that his brother Johnny was living
somewhere in this vast cavern, did not console him. So he
stalked moodily to his room in the barracks, shut the door,
sat down heavily on the sole chair, cupped his chin in his
hand, and brooded.

After a while he got up, and stood by the window,
staring out at the rolling landscape and the luminous silver
sky. And, as he stared, the sky suddenly paled and
darkened. Within a minute's time, night reigned outside,
peppered with the twinkling lights of distant villages and
scattered farms, although overhead there was a dense black
void without a single star. Cathcart groped his way back
through the darkness until he found and snapped on the
light switch. Then he glanced at his wristwatch—just a
minute or two after six o'clock. A gong rang in the
corridor. Cathcart opened his door and looked out. The
corridor was lighted, and colonists were emerging from
their rooms.

"What's going on?" he asked of a freckle¬-faced young

man about his own age who was just coming down the hall.

"Grub, I guess," the other replied, holding out his hand and grinning engagingly. "Name's Mick—I mean Paul Smith. What's yours?"

"Robert Cathcart. Didn't I see you in the elevator?"

Smith's grin broadened. "Mustn't call it an elevator. Teacher says it's an 'atom disintegrator.' "

"If you mean the Inspector, I believe he called it a 'status-changing machine.' "

Smith laughed. "I knew it was something quite impossible. Well, ain't we got fun. Are we all crazy, or what?"

"I guess 'what' is the answer," Cathcart soberly replied. "Facilis descensus Averni."

"Come again?"

"That's Latin. It's from Virgil. It's the first part of a famous quotation that goes: 'Easy is the descent into hell, but to retrace one's steps, and regain the world above, this is the difficulty, this the labor.'"

Smith whistled admiringly. "What a swell lead for a news story…"

"You aren't by any chance a reporter?"

Smith jumped guiltily. Then turned large blue eyes reproachfully at his accuser. "Why, you know perfectly well that 'the Boss' won't tolerate reporters."

JUST then they reached a pair of closed double doors surmounted by a large sign reading: "DINING HALL." In front of the doors stood a group of about twenty men, waiting there in their black uniforms, with the red shoulder-insignia of the Colony Guards. One of these Cathcart recognized as Putorius Terro, the truck driver who had been with him in New Jersey earlier that afternoon.

Terro broke away from the group and stepped over. "Hello!" he said truculently. "Where have you been all this while?"

"All this while?" Cathcart echoed. "What do you mean? I got here this afternoon."

"What held you up? I've been here for the last four days." He stepped up very close to Cathcart and thrust some folded papers into his hand, at the same time whispering into his ear, "Just shove these papers into your pocket, and don't look at them until you get back to your room. They'll give you the low-down about this new universe."

He moved away through the crowd of colonists.

"Pleasant-looking friend you have there," Smith remarked with a grimace. "What did he whisper in your ear?"

"Now I'm sure that you're a reporter," Cathcart countered evasively, thrusting the packet of papers into his breeches pocket.

Just then a disturbance in the crowd behind them attracted their attention. It looked like fisticuffs at first glance. One of the colonists, a dark-complexioned man in overalls, was struggling in the hands of two of the guards.

"But I tella you, I no passa da pape," he cried.

"What's your name?" snapped one of the guards.

"Tony Angelino."

"Well, Tony, who passed the paper to you?"

Angelino looked wildly around for someone on whom to put the blame.

Terro stepped up to the group. "It was him there," he announced, pointing his finger at Cathcart. "I saw him."

"Why, you—!" Cathcart indignantly began.

"Sì! Sì!" exclaimed Tony, delighted at finding a scapegoat. "He passa me da pape."

Cathcart wheeled about in surprise to face his second accuser.

But now Terro cried, "Search him!" And Cathcart was promptly seized and held by two of the guards without any real struggle. Terro, slight smile on his face, then reached into Cathcart's pocket, and pulled out the package of papers. "Political leaflets! Populistic propaganda!" he triumphantly shouted.

"Why, you yourself—" Cathcart began. Then something stayed his tongue. Shrugging his broad shoulders resignedly, he lamely explained to his captors, "These papers—they are not mine. Someone thrust them into my pocket just now. I—I am a chemist, not a politician."

"Well that's a likely story if I've ever heard one," sneered a burly-looking Sergeant, bustling up. "Come on, you men, take him over to Headquarters on the double."

Cathcart then turned to Smith, who had been watching the whole performance with a big, broad grin on his freckled Irish face. "Come along and vouch for me."

But Smith shook his head. "Sorry," he replied, "but I never saw you until a few moments ago."

"Better pinch him, too," the swarthy rat-faced Terro suggested. "He might very well be one of the Populists, too."

"Okay, you take him," the Sergeant commanded Terro.

So, protesting, Smith was dragged along.

Behind them the dining room doors were just opening to admit a lengthy line of hungry colonists to the hot supper that the two prisoners were going to miss. The prisoners were hastily escorted through the night over to the Administration Building, then on down into its basement where they were then thrust unceremoniously into a cell.

CHAPTER THREE
Aren't We Still on Earth?

AS THE guards departed after locking the two of them in their cell, Smith turned reproachfully to Cathcart with, "Nice mess you've got me into!" But there was a twinkle in his blue eyes, which belied his tone of voice.

"Oho!" Cathcart replied. "You don't seem particularly despondent. What's up?"

"Well," laughed Smith, "the truth is that I rather welcome this arrest. Maybe now I'll find out some of the things I came here to learn."

"Such as?"

"The location of Malcolm Frain's alleged colonies, and what becomes of the thousands of people who disappear into them."

"I'm on the same quest myself," Cathcart admitted, "but not for any newspaper."

"Who said anything about a newspaper?" Smith hotly retorted.

"Oh, I'll keep your secret."

"But I haven't any secret."

"All right, pal, you haven't any secret; and I have a selfish reason for not giving you away. I'm here looking for my brother, and I'd hate to have my quest interrupted by getting suspected of being a friend of a newshawk."

"Have it your own way," Smith retorted, grinning.

They lapsed into silence. Cathcart turning over in his mind the rapid succession of the events of the day, and wondering how Putorius Terra, who had left the earth only an hour or two ahead (although claiming to have arrived here four days ahead), had so speedily been made a regular member of the colony guards, and had become so soon involved in political propaganda. Why, indeed, should there be political propaganda in a utopia?

His thoughts were interrupted by the arrival of two guards, who unlocked the cell door, and commanded, "Hey, you in the black uniform, come with us."

"Good-bye," waved Smith. "Invite me to the hanging."

The two soldiers scowled at him, as they led Cathcart away, upstairs to an office on the ground floor, where a stern-faced Inspector sat behind a desk. The two guards halted their prisoner in front of the desk.

"Name Cathcart?" snapped the official.

"Yes, Sir."

"Charged with possessing Populistic literature?"

"So I understand, but it was planted on me."

"A likely story. You were warned not to have anything to do with any investigations of the nature of this new universe, were you not?"

"So that's what those papers were about? I haven't read them yet."

"Answer my question!"

"No. No one warned me. The Inspector who lectured to us seemed quite willing to answer questions on the subject, and said nothing whatever about not pursuing the subject further."

"Well, you know the rule now. And the penalty is a year's hard labor on the roads. Who gave you the subversive literature that was found on you?"

Just then a guardsman bustled in and announced, "Important message, Sir," and then whispered something in the Inspector's ear. Cathcart caught "…message from outside…Boss's daughter…"

"Not so loud, you fool!"

More whispering. The Inspector's already severe face contorted into a scowl. Finally he turned to Cathcart with, "Young man, your explanation will be accepted—for the present." Then to one of the guards, "Take this fellow to Dr. Freundlich's house."

THE guard led Cathcart out into the starless tropic night, and down a brightly-lighted street, past store windows and a motion picture theater, to a residence district, where he mounted the steps of a rather pretentious stone dwelling, and rang the doorbell. The maid who answered the door gasped, glanced hurriedly from the guard to Cathcart, fell back a step, and crossed herself.

"Is the Professor in?" the guard gruffly inquired.

"Y—yes, Sir. Won't you come in?"

"Come on, fellow," said the guard, striding into the house.

In the hallway stood a bullet-headed roly-poly man with closely cropped hair and thick-lensed glasses. His smooth features displayed concern, tinged with fear.

"What—what is it, officers?" he mildly inquired.

"Only one of us is an officer," snapped the guard. "This fellow here is paroled into your custody, Professor, by order of Inspector Jenks. Name—¬Cathcart. That's all." He turned and stamped out of the house.

"Ah, my friend, and what is your crime?" asked the little man, solicitously.

"As far as I can make out," Cathcart replied a bit doubtfully, "I am charged with possessing seditious literature, though I swear it was planted on me. I arrived in this colony only a few hours ago, and haven't had time enough to find out what to be seditious about, even if I wanted to. May I ask if you are Herr Doktor Emanuel K. Freundlich?"

"But yes, of course. You have heard of me, no? And do the people back on Earth still remember my work on atomic physics?"

"Why not? It is scarcely two months since your thesis was published, shortly after I started working for Frain."

"Ach, no. That was five years ago. My thesis, I mean. And you, you are not by any chance the young Robert Cathcart, Ph. D. from Johns Hopkins, who was working for the Chemical Foundation at about the same time?"

"I am Robert Cathcart, and I worked for the Foundation, but not five years ago. Five years ago I was still at Harvard, and hadn't even started my postgraduate work at Johns Hopkins."

Dr. Freundlich took off his thick-lensed glasses and rubbed his watery blue eyes with a tired gesture. "Ach, it is that verdammte time—difference between your universe and ours!" he exclaimed in an exasperated tone. "What date was it when you left Earth? ¬But no, no," holding up one pudgy hand, "you must not answer me. It is verboten—prohibited—against the law. By the way, have you dined?"

"No." Cathcart replied, with a wry face. "They arrested me just as the dining room doors were about to open."

The little professor beamed. "Ah, then you are just in time. Minna, O Minna! Set another place at the table. And now, my dear young friend, tell me all about your unfortunate experiences." He led his guest into a sitting room, and offered him a chair.

CATHCART began his story at the beginning—the disappearance of his brother.

"Ah," commented Dr. Freundlich, "as Omar says:

> *'Strange, is it not? that of the myriads who*
> *before us pass'd the door of Darkness through,*
> *not one returns to tell us of the Road,*
> *which to discover we must travel too.'*

Well, let us hope that now you shall discover. Proceed."

So Cathcart continued with his story. Dr. Freundlich's kind face clouded at the account of the brutality in the elevator, or "status-changing machine," or whatever; and again at the planting of the documents on Cathcart, and his resulting arrest. But at the end of the story, Freundlich's expression changed to an inscrutable one, which Cathcart found it hard to fathom.

"Ach, it does not hold water, quite. Too quickly you are arrested, and too soon released. I fear that you are an 'agent provocateur'—that you are sent to spy upon me. But you will find that old Herr Freundlich is thoroughly loyal to the Boss—thoroughly."

"Do they suspect everyone?" Cathcart indignantly exclaimed. "This place was described to me as a utopia. Certainly the outline of your laws and living conditions that the Inspector gave us in the brief lecture this afternoon sounded absolutely idyllic. Why then should there be communism and rebellion here?"

Freundlich peered inquiringly through his thick glasses. "When God made Paradise, he put a snake there too," he reminded.

Cathcart smiled. "So you blame Malcolm Frain for this unrest?"

"No, no! I did not mean that. Please! If you are going to arrest me, do so now, before my sister enters."

"I don't know what on earth you mean. I am not a spy—merely a colonist, hoping to learn from you what this is all about."

"You'll learn nothing from me! It is verboten. Ach, too late! Here comes my sister." A placid blonde Teutonic lady of uncertain age was entering the room. "Emily, this is young Dr. Cathcart, who has been assigned by the Boss to assist me in my laboratories."

Comprehension dawned in Cathcart's face. "Why, of course!" he exclaimed.

"And what else would you be here for, my young friend?" Freundlich blandly replied. "You see, Emily, he is a bit of a dummkopf. I shall have to teach him much."

"Do not make fun of the poor young man, Emmanuel," his sister reproved him, as they walked into the dining room.

At the meal the conversation soon developed into a cross-examination of the younger man as to developments in atomic physics in the alleged five years since Dr. Freundlich left the Earth, the Herr Doktor expressing repeated surprise at the apparent total lack of progress during that period.

After dinner, Cathcart's belongings arrived by messenger, and he was shown to the guestroom of the Freundlichs.

In the morning his host beamingly informed him that word had arrived from Headquarters withdrawing all charges, and definitely assigning Cathcart as the doctor's assistant. "So perhaps you are not an 'agent provocateur,' after all."

But, in spite of this last remark, Dr. Freundlich

continued to draw the line at any discussion of the nature of this new cellular universe in which the colony was supposed to constitute one of the holes.

CATHCART'S first day at his new job was spent in getting an advance in pay, buying some civilian clothes, learning the ropes of his host's laboratory, and picking up the threads of the various problems of industrial chemistry on which his host was engaged. But all the time, under the cover of an intent interest in what the roly-poly little Prussian was telling him, Cathcart's keen gray eyes' were always searching for clues—for he felt instinctively that Dr. Freundlich was holding something back from him.

And Cathcart found clues aplenty. Among the laboratory equipment, which showed signs of recent use, were an Atwood's machine, a simple pendulum, a magnetic compass, and a Foucault pendulum, none of which had any possible application to any problem on which Dr. Freundlich had been supposed to be working. These set Cathcart to thinking, for every one of these four items could be used to ascertain some feature of the nature of the physical universe. But, inasmuch as the Herr Doktor had refused to talk on the subject, Cathcart merely grinned to himself and held his peace for the present.

The next day—to Cathcart's great surprise—was Sunday. He had left Frain City, New Jersey, in the "status changing machine," on a Monday at 8:30 p. m.; and, after a twenty minute trip, had arrived at this colony at 4:15 p. m.—on what day of the week or month, he had not thought to ask. And now, two days later, it was Sunday!

Oh, well. Perhaps a day off would give him his long-awaited chance to resume his search for his brother. He broached the matter to his host and hostess at breakfast.

"Do we have to work today?"

"No."

"Then could it be arranged somehow for me to get to Town 13, to hunt for Johnny?"

"It could be, yah," dubiously. "We could hire a Frain V-8. All cars here belong to the government, but are very cheap to hire. A most excellent arrangement. But the office in Town 13 would not be open on a Sunday. So let us work this afternoon, and then take Monday afternoon for the trip, which is but thirty miles."

"Will tomorrow be Monday?" Cathcart asked.

"And why not?" Dr. Freundlich replied. Then, catching the twinkle in Cathcart's eye. "Ah, I see that you jest. But you must not jest, my young friend. It is verboten to poke fun at anything¬ that the Boss has ordained."

"Meaning Malcolm Frain?"

"Yes. But it is also verboten to call him anything other than 'The Boss' down here."

Miss Freundlich, a puzzled frown on her bland blonde face, interposed, "What else could day after today be than Monday?"

"Shhh, Emily!" cautioned Dr. Freundlich. "Enough of this jesting. Our young friend might report us."

And, in spite of Cathcart's protestations that he was not a spy, the Freundlichs refused to discuss the matter further.

HE ATTENDED church with his hosts, devout Lutherans, and worked that afternoon and the next morning in the laboratory. Monday, right after lunch, the three of them set out in a hired car on an excellent concrete highway that wound across the level plain directly away from the high wall of white rock against which lay the capital city. Above them stretched an unbroken expanse of luminous pearly white clouds. The Herr Doktor drove.

Cathcart, sitting in the front seat beside him, stared aloft for some time; then said, "This sunless rainless sky gets me down. Doesn't it ever change?"

"Never except at night," Freundlich asserted.

Cathcart shuddered. "It gives me the creeps."

A bit further on, they came upon a detour sign and a gang of men in striped overalls, working with picks and shovels, and guarded by a squad of black-uniformed colony guards. As Freundlich was about to turn into the side road, the Corporal in charge looked up. It was Putorius Terro!

"Halt!" he shouted. Then to his squad, "Arrest that man. He's an escaped convict."

"Aber nein!" Dr. Freundlich exclaimed, as he stopped the car. His pale eyes flashed behind his thick-lensed glasses, and his short-cropped hair seemed to brittle belligerently. "He has been paroled to me."

"Have you the parole papers with you?"

"No, but—"

"Get out of the car, all three of you."

Cathcart's face was calm, but his eyes were dangerous. "This car is rented in my name, Terro," he said in level tones. "Would they let a criminal rent a state car?" He held out the rental slip.

"Oh, I beg your pardon, Bob," Terro apologized in an oily voice. "Come over here a minute." Then he whispered, "I was only doing my duty. Have to throw a bluff, you know. Thanks for not telling who planted the papers on you the other day. I shan't forget. How did you beat the rap?"

"I guess they needed a chemist more than they needed a man for the chain gang." Cathcart glanced around, and his eye fell on a small redheaded freckle-faced grinning convict. "Oh, hello, Smith."

"Real name's Mickey Foley," the convict replied, his grin broadening. "Reporter for the New York Daily Tabloid. They caught me red-handed. But civilians mustn't talk to prisoners, must they, Corporal?"

"No, you really shouldn't Bob," Terro confirmed. "Well, see you later."

Cathcart, Dr. Freundlich, and the latter's stolid blonde sister clambered back into the car, and were on their way.

"Who is your scowling Corporal friend?" Dr. Freundlich asked.

"His name is Putorius Terro. He—"

"Ah! Putorius is the Latin word for weasel, and Terro is the proprietary name for a certain brand of poison. He will bear watching."

"He's not to blame for his name, but it certainly fits. I knew him quite well on Earth; we were truck drivers together. And, unless he has changed a lot, he is a radical and a troublemaker."

THEIR course finally veered to the right, and another towering wall of their cellular world loomed ahead. Against it nestled a pretty little town of about two thousand inhabitants, and several factories. Dr. Freundlich stopped the car in the public square in front of a two-story brick building, flying the red "F" in a white circle on a blue field. No Stars and Stripes alongside of it as on Earth, for here the Boss was supreme, and acknowledged no higher power.

Cathcart's heart sped up as he and Dr. Freundlich mounted the steps. To the Sergeant at the desk inside, the Doctor said, "My young friend here is looking for his brother, named John Cathcart."

The Sergeant shook his head. "No such person since I've been here." He lumbered to his feet, and began pawing in a card-file. "Ah, here's his record. 'John Cathcart, agricultural foreman. Height, five feet eleven. Weight—"

"Skip it!" Cathcart impatiently cut in. "Where is he?"

"'—160 pounds,'" the unperturbed Sergeant continued. "'Eyes, blue. Hair, brown.'"

"Skip it!"

The Sergeant looked up annoyedly. "All right. All right. Your brother was transferred here from another colony about three years ago, as head foreman of all the government farms of this district. He died two years ago. Tractor upset on him. Age 36."

"But it can't be!" Cathcart exclaimed. "Johnny was only 21 when he left the Earth six months ago!"

"Does the description fit?" Dr. Freundlich asked, with kindly concern in his watery eyes.

"Yes, except his weight. He weighed only 132, the last time I saw him."

"But in fifteen years he could—"

"What do you mean? Fifteen years?"

"You forget the time-discrepancy."

So Johnny was dead. Cathcart blinked away a tear.

Then, straightening up, he resolutely announced, "Well, here ends my quest. Now to get back to the Earth."

Dr. Freundlich gazed sadly at him. "My dear young friend, there is no going back."

"How absurd!" Cathcart exclaimed. "I made very clear, when I signed up, that I wanted merely to find my brother. Surely they won't—they can't—keep me here against my will."

"The Boss can and will do whatever he pleases. He is omnipotent in this, his colony."

"Then I say, damn Boss Frain!" For a moment Cathcart clenched his fists. But gradually the look of rage in his face changed to a frightened caged expression.

With a groan he sunk upon a chair, and took his face in his hands.

CHAPTER FOUR
The Nature of the Universe

A HAND was laid on his crumpled shoulders, and the kind voice of Dr. Freundlich said, "Careful, son, careful... I know how you feel. But in your sudden grief and despair, take care to utter no treason."

But it was not the doctor's words that brought Cathcart out of his daze. Rather it was the thought of the flaming Donna Frain, and her projected visits to this colony.

Cathcart shook himself together and stood up. "Thank you, Sir." Then looking the Sergeant squarely in the eye, "I have no cause for treason. Where is my brother buried?"

The official directed them to the local cemetery, where they purchased a wreath of flowers and placed it on Johnny's stone. As Cathcart knelt beside the grave, and read his brother's birth date in outer world notation, he gave up all hope that this might be some ghastly mistake— some other John Cathcart than his brother. And also all hope of ever seeing the outer world again himself.

Emily Freundlich laid a motherly hand on Cathcart's shoulder. Dr. Freundlich, shaking his head sadly, began, "'For some we loved, the loveliest and the best—'"

"Please don't," Cathcart begged.

As the three of them drove back together to the capital city, the little Prussian said, "My young friend, I no longer suspect you. Your grief and your horror have been too genuine. I trust you now. Let us cooperate and search for the secret key to this universe."

"Careful, Emmanuel!" his sister interposed. "This is treason."

Dr. Freundlich exploded, "Let it be treason, then! I believe we can trust Mr. Cathcart here. There may be some escape from Malcolm Frain, if we can once discover the secret of this cockeyed universe of his."

"I'm with you, Sir," Cathcart asserted. "What have you found out so far?"

"Um," Freundlich replied, pursing up his pudgy lips. "I have measured 'g,' the acceleration of gravity, with both Atwood's machine and a simple pendulum—a compound one, of course—and have obtained exactly the Earth value: 32.16 feet per second per second. This would indicate that we are still on Earth, in a cavern not very far below the surface, reached by the elevator, which the authorities call a 'status-changing machine.'"

But Cathcart objected. "You've been here for five years, you say, Doctor. Yet the warehouse from which we both came here, hadn't been built that far back. In fact, when I was carting silt into it in a motor-truck three months ago, there was not even a hole in the ground for an elevator shaft."

"You forget the time-discrepancy."

"Damn the time-discrepancy! And yet— Hold on a minute. According to my reckoning, you were on Earth two months ago; according to yours, you've been here five years. Terro preceded me here by only three hours and yet said that he had been here four days. My brother—" His voice caught, then continued, "grew fifteen years older in six months. I wonder if, after all, there may not be some fixed ratio, thirty to one, between our time and that of the real world."

"A mere coincidence, I'm afraid," said Freundlich,

shaking his bullet head, "and I doubt if we are on the Earth anyway, in spite of 'g;' for the magnetic compass indicates no north, and the plane of my Foucault pendulum shifts imperceptibly, instead of making one complete rotation each 24 hours as it ought to." *

"Just what is the rate of shift that you have observed here?"

"About half a degree an hour."

"There!" Cathcart exclaimed triumphantly. "That's the same thirty-to-one ratio between our time and Earth time. The failure of the compass can perhaps be explained by iron deposits in the walls of this cavern. I believe that we're on the Earth, with merely our time sped up in some manner."

But again Dr. Freundlich shook his round head. "If that were so," said he, "then 'g' would appear to have only one one-thousandth of the Earth value, instead of exactly the Earth value. Things when dropped would merely float down to the ground, instead of falling. A man could unbelievably jump a billion times as high as he can now.

---

* The Foucault pendulum was invented by Jean Bernard Leon Foucault, a French physicist in 1851. By means of this instrument, he demonstrated the rotation of the Earth on its axis by the diurnal rotation plane of oscillation of a long pendulum with a heavy weight. The following year he invented the gyroscope. He was one of the most brilliant of French physicists, and was first to prove that light travels slower in water than in air. He also invented the polarizing prism and discovered a means of giving the mirrors of reflecting telescopes the form of a spheroid or paraboloid of revolution. —Ed.

No, my young friend, we bark up the wrong tree, I'm afraid."

"And I'm afraid," his blonde sister cut in from the back seat, "that we'll all end up in jail if you two men don't stop discussing verboten matters!"

DURING the weeks that followed, they resumed the discussion from time to time. And, whenever they were sure not to be interrupted by anyone who knew enough physics to suspect them, they repeated and verified their experiments. Their regular—and supposedly only—work consisted mostly of dyestuffs and military explosives. Why the military explosives, Cathcart often wondered? But, high though Dr. Freundlich stood in the councils of the Frain Industries, the doctor could not enlighten him.

Several months after his arrival, Cathcart suffered two annoyances. The first was to see the insufferable Putorius Terro, now promoted to Sergeant, escorting the flaming Donna Frain on the streets of the capital city. When Cathcart had stepped forward eagerly to greet her, he had imagined that for a moment her eyes too lit up. But swiftly they had become cold green and inscrutable, and she had snapped, "Cathcart, have a care! Civilian colonists do not speak to Inspectors unless spoken to."

Then she had passed on with head held high, and Sergeant Terro had grinned back possessively and tauntingly over his shoulder.

And that same day Cathcart had received a notice to don his uniform and report for military duty. Dr. Freundlich explained that every able-bodied male was liable to one week's duty as a soldier, out of every month.

"What I can't see," Cathcart exploded, "is why Malcolm Frain—I mean 'the Boss'—has to have all this army. It's many times more than enough to keep order here, and certainly there's no danger of any attack on this colony. Though I suppose the Boss does have a purpose in everything he does."

"It is not for us to question his purposes, my young friend," Freundlich sententiously replied. Then, glancing shrewdly at Cathcart, he added, "But I think that the real cause of your annoyance is not the military establishment of the Boss, but rather the military establishment of the Boss's daughter, Donna Frain. I've noted that young weasel...Terro...about town here, and he seems to be a devil with the ladies."

Cathcart flushed. Then the color gradually drained from his cheeks, and his broad shoulders slumped.

Freundlich stepped over to his shelves of chemicals, took down a large glass jug and poured out a tumblerful of ruby colored liquids. "Here, drink this. It will make you feel better."

"What is it?"

"Wine."

"But I thought that liquor was forbidden by the Boss."

"It is. But one of the advantages of being a chemist is that I can make wine synthetically. Terro has irked you. 'Oh, many a Cup of this forbidden Wine must drown the memory of that insolence!' as old Omar used to say."

Cathcart took the glass, and drained it.

Freundlich continued, "Now go to your drill; and, when you see Terro, face him with a smile. Meanwhile I'll putter around here, and complete our gyrocompass. If there's any north in this cellular world, a gyrocompass, being immune to iron deposits, ought to show it."

Cathcart put on the black uniform that he had worn as a truck driver on Earth and reported at the headquarters building, where the red shoulder¬-insignia of the Colony Guards were sewed on, and he was put in a company of about a hundred green recruits, who were then marched to barracks in a nearby village.

THE first six days of the week were spent in drilling, rifle and revolver shooting, and instruction in military courtesies. But on the seventh day (the extra day of the eight day week, known as Frainday) they were given actual work to do, guarding road gangs. And among Cathcart's prisoners was Mickey Foley, alias Paul Smith, the tabloid reporter from New York.

"Well, well," exclaimed Foley, beaming, as he saw who had been placed over him. "If it isn't the criminal syndicalist! And to think that if it hadn't been for your good luck and my poor luck, I might be guarding you, as Damon Runyan said in 'Pilgrim's Progress.' Mind if I ask you a question?"

Cathcart grinned back. "If it isn't for newspaper purposes, nor treasonable."

"How would I be sending a story to my paper from here? I ask you!"

"Then it is treasonable?"

"Sure it's treasonable! How much does the surface of the Earth curve?"

"About eight inches to a mile. But I can't see that there's anything treasonable about that."

"Well, stop me if you've heard this one. I've been helping the surveyors run levels for this road, and this world is practically flat. Wouldn't that make a hit with Bryan!"

"Bryan is dead."

"Well, so'll you be, if you're caught talking science with

a newspaper man. But, all joking aside, I think there's a story in this, somehow."

"I wouldn't be surprised," Cathcart admitted, his gray eyes narrowing thoughtfully.

That evening, his tour of duty over, he reported this information to Dr. Freundlich, and the Herr Doktor reported in return that his gyrocompass had indicated as north the same direction as in the warehouse from which they had entered this cellular world, and also that the Foucault pendulum rotated at a rate of exactly 11° 15′ per day.

But the importance of these scientific developments was completely overshadowed by the political news of the past week. The object of the visit of Inspector Donna Frain to this colony, as the direct representative of her father, had become known. The circulating of leaflets criticizing the Boss had reached sudden and unexpected new heights, discontent was seething, and the flaming Donna had come to take personal charge of the espionage work of the dread Frain Secret Service. Her constant military escort was Sergeant Terro.

"I don't think that he's enough protection for her," Cathcart declared.

"Meaning that you'd like to go along too?" asked Dr. Freundlich, smiling shrewdly.

"No. I don't butt in where I'm not wanted. But all the same, the Boss's daughter ought to be guarded by a full squad of dependable men."

"To chaperone the Weasel?"

Cathcart made a wry face. "Maybe that's what I do mean, after all," he admitted. "So let's skip it."

"No," Freundlich objected. "I think that you are really sincere in your desire to protect the Boss's daughter. The

Inspector in Charge here has tried to prevail on her to accept additional guards, but she has refused. They can't even give secret protection to her, for she herself commands the Secret Service. So I suggest that you trail the two of them, not to spy upon your enemy, but rather to protect your friend. You have my permission to leave your laboratory work for that purpose."

THE next day was Sunday, Donna Frain, accompanied by the inevitable Terro, attended Episcopal services; and Robert Cathcart, with the full approval of the Freundlichs, also went to the Episcopal Cathedral, instead of to the Lutheran church with his host and hostess.

After the service, Donna and her escort set out on foot for the city limits, and Cathcart trailed them. The couple entered a dense thicket of five-year-old pines and hardwood along the sheer face of the barrier cliff, and Cathcart continued to follow them. They seemed to be rather aimlessly following a winding trail, rather than to be bound for any particular destination.

Finally the path widened out into a little clearing, carpeted with soft club moss, Donna and the Sergeant sat down together on the moss. Cathcart hid behind a bush at the edge of the wood, and peered out.

He was rapidly becoming more and more ashamed of his role of spy, as he gradually admitted to himself that, after all, his major interest was to protect Donna Frain from Putorius Terro, rather than from the enemies of the realm.

But thus far Terro did not appear to be acting in any way inconsistent with his apparent position as bodyguard and servitor to the daughter of the Boss. Only the burning light in Terro's eyes, as they devoured the lovely Donna, belied his apparent subordinate position. Cathcart turned his head away, to blot out the unwelcome sight.

Suddenly Donna screamed!

Cathcart leaped to his feet, and dashed out into the clearing.

From the woods on the opposite side, straight toward Donna and Terro, there was rushing a fearsome many-legged silver-colored jointed beast, about forty feet in length and five feet high. Its motion was a cross between a gallop and a wriggle, as it covered the ground with prodigious speed.

Donna and Terro were both now on their feet, Terro adding his frightened yell to Donna's shrieks, as he crashed blindly into her in his frantic rush for safety.

Terro's blind rush pushed Donna out of the path of the charging monstrosity. Both he and she stumbled and fell headlong into the soft moss. The beast kept on. And, unarmed though Cathcart was, he ran to meet it.

But it never reached him. Suddenly it halted, shuddered, and settled heavily to the ground, as though machinery within it had run down. Cathcart's rush carried him on, to bump against the huge inert remains. It felt soft and crinkly, like tinsel over papier-mâché. His hands and the front of his suit, where he had touched the creature, were covered with silver dust, as if from poorly applied aluminum paint. Could it be that this beast, which a moment before had seemed to be a menacing monstrosity, was nothing more than a mere carnival creation impelled by machinery? But no; it had been too real for that.

These thoughts flashed through Cathcart's mind in an instant; his real concern was for Donna Frain. Turning quickly, he picked her up from where she had fallen. "Are you all right?" he asked.

Still quivering, she clung to him. A fierce joy surged through him, as he held her close. She looked up into his eyes for a brief instant, and seemed content.

"Hi, there!" shouted Terro, scrambling to his feet.

Cathcart released the girl, flushed guiltily, and clenched his fists.

BUT DONNA had regained her poise. With gratitude shining in her green eyes—warm green now, rather than their usual jade inscrutability, she exclaimed, "You two men have saved my life! You, Sergeant Terro, pushed me out of the path of the charging monster just in time; and you, Private Cathcart, killed the monster. This will go well on the records of both of you."

Cathcart's eyes flashed, as he opened his mouth to protest that Terro had run like a coward and had merely accidentally stumbled against Donna in his mad flight. But, before the words came out, he clamped his jaws together again, grinned irritatingly, and held up his right arm in salute.

"A pleasure to be of service, Inspector," he said.

Putorius Terro was not so tactful. "Cathcart didn't even touch the beast," he blurted out.

"No?" asked Cathcart, amusement glinting in his gray eyes, as he spread his arms wide, disclosing the silver powder smeared all over the front of him. Then, with a sudden contempt for letting himself be put in the same class as his impostor rival, "The Sergeant speaks the truth. I admit to a foolhardy attempt to kill the monster with my bare hands, but apparently the dying was the monster's own idea."

Donna imperiously shook her flaming head. "You are too modest, Private Cathcart," she declared. "I saw what I saw. But now we have a problem on our hands. I must pledge you two men to secrecy, for—for—for it would never do for the colonists to know that this utopia has harbored a nightmare creature like this. Cathcart, stay here in this clearing and see that no one comes near the body. You, Sergeant—"

"But, Inspector," Terro interrupted, "I tell you— Well, anyway, what was Cathcart doing trailing us? Ask him that."

"I will attend to that question later! But, as I was saying—"

"You might just as well hear the answer now," Cathcart cut in. "I was trailing you because I feared that there might be Populists in this wood, and I felt that the daughter of the Boss was entitled to more of a bodyguard than just one Sergeant."

"Why you—" Terro began.

"Silence!" Donna snapped. "Sergeant, come with me. You will guard the entrance to the wood, while I go to get additional troops, to throw a cordon around the place. Also for a truck, to remove the carcass."

She and Terro started off down the trail together toward town. Cathcart grinned after them, and Terro flashed back at him a black look, which gradually merged into one of triumph.

Cathcart shrugged his broad shoulders; then turned his attention to the dead silver-colored monster. Where had he seen something like this before? In carnivals? At the Mardi Gras? In dreams? No. That was not it. Some obscure thought clamored for entrance at the threshold of his mind.

He walked around the carcass, kicking it once or twice. Silver dust powdered his shoe. He noted a light silver trail on the moss and grass, leading back the way the beast had come.

SNAPPING his fingers with sudden resolution, he dogtrotted down this back trail. A few hundred yards led him to the barrier wall of this pocket in solid space, which housed the colony. The wall towered above him, gray-white and flat and sheer, clear to the clouds, and at its foot flanked with bushes and climbing vines. Into a thicket led the silver trail; and as Cathcart parted the shrubbery with his hands, he saw that the cliff-face beyond was riven—a jagged crack some twenty feet high, and five or six feet wide at the base. This then was the lair from which the silver beast had emerged.

On inspecting this opening more carefully, Cathcart saw that its faint penciled line extended up the barrier until lost to view in the mists above. At its base it had forked, and the triangular piece of rock formed by the fork had been forced out and was lying in the bushes to one side.

Cathcart peered into the dark and cavernous hole. Did its blackness hide other silver beasts? Well, he must take the chance. For if, as he had been told by the lecturer on his first day in this colony, it was true that this new world was a part of a cellular universe, might not this cave lead to another cell? Perhaps he, Robert Cathcart, might discover new worlds for Malcolm Frain to conquer, and thus gain credit—perhaps even freedom from his imprisonment! At least, he might possibly learn something of interest and assistance to the scientific speculations of himself and Dr. Freundlich. So, taking a paper of matches from his pocket, he lit one, and groped his way in.

The rock underfoot was jagged and rough, with many projections man-high stalagmites, it seemed. He had progressed only about a hundred yards when half his matches gave out; so he retraced his steps. Then ran back through the woods to the clearing, lest Donna Frain return in time to discover that he had been exploring.

Just in time, too, for a few minutes later Putorius Terro emerged from the woods on the side toward the town.

"Where's the boss?" Cathcart innocently asked, but his gray eyes held hidden amusement.

"You mean the Boss's daughter."

"Have it your own way," Cathcart shrugged.

"She'll be bringing a truck. I have posted troops all around the wood. No one but the three of us are to come in here, or know of this. And now, Cathcart, before she gets here, I want to tell you a few things I've got on my mind. You need to lay off of Donna Frain and me. If you poke your grinning face into my affairs again, I'll frame you and get you put onto roadwork, or perhaps something worse. I have considerable influence with the Administration—"

"So I see."

"—and in other quarters," Terro added meaningly. "So watch out…"

"Terro, I don't altogether trust your loyalty to the Boss, and— Shhh! Here comes Inspector Donna."

A large auto-truck then crashed its way into the clearing and stopped. Donna clambered out of the driver's seat, and directed the two men to take axes, shovels and tarpaulins out of the back, chop up the carcass, load the pieces aboard, and cover the mess with tarpaulins.

The pieces were singularly light and pithy, but were real insect flesh.

Watching for his opportunity, Cathcart discovered a large electric flashlight in a pocket of one of the doors of the truck. While no one was looking, he dropped it into the tall grass.

When the entire mess had been loaded aboard, Donna hopped back into the truck, turned it around, and drove it out of the woods, followed by Terro and Cathcart on foot.

"Remember what I warned you," said Terro in a low voice.

"The same goes for you," Cathcart replied.

Upon reaching the open fields beyond the woods, Donna ordered Sergeant Terro to gather up the guards, while she herself set out alone for Headquarters with the truck.

"Mind you, both of you, not a word of this episode to anyone," was her parting admonition.

CATHCART found himself alone. Now was his chance! Rushing back into the wood, he retrieved the flashlight from the tall grass, and hurried to the crack in the barrier cliff.

When he was well inside of the cavern, he flashed his light completely around him. Far above him towered the crack, which widened out considerably within the face of the wall.

Slowly and painfully he picked his way inward. The floor became more and more rough, the cavern wider and wider, although not too wide for the beam of his lamp to reach both sides.

At last, after about a mile of clambering around and over stalagmites, a billowy black curtain blocked the entire passage.

There was something unreal, unsubstantial, intangible about that curtain! The ray of Cathcart's electric torch, when played upon it, stopped abruptly, but neither penetrated nor illumined it. He approached it slowly, with great care, and reached out his hand to touch it. Amazingly, his hand passed through it, into it, without feeling it whatsoever. It was a black mist, light absorbing! Cathcart recoiled.

But, though impervious to light, the black mist was not impervious to sound. From beyond it Cathcart could hear a slow, almost musical, deep rumble, which rose and fell in uneven waves.

As he stood irresolute in the face of this new phenomenon, he noticed a slightly red tinge to the beam of his electric flash—the batteries had begun to fail. Turning panic-stricken, he ran stumbling back along the way that he had come.

Paler and redder grew the glow of his lamp. He switched it off, and staggered a few steps in jet-black darkness. Then hurriedly switched it on again, lest he get turned around.

For seeming hours this continued, until the dull red glow became practically useless. A long wait was indicated, in the forlorn hope that the battery might pick up again. But in his next short grope-ahead, he crashed full into a pillar of stone, and the electric torch was dashed from his grasp.

On hands and knees he felt about for it; and, just as he was despairing, found it again. But, when he pressed the button, no light came. He tried it several times than ran his fingers all over it—the lens was gone, and the bulb smashed.

With a wild moan he sprang to his feet. Then halted.

"You fool!" he cried aloud. "No panic now!"

But which way was out? While groping for the torch, he had lost all sense of direction!

CHAPTER FIVE
The World of the Giants

LOST! Without a light, in the jet black darkness of the caverns of the silver beast! Without even an idea of which direction was out!

Cathcart sat heavily down on a rounded stalagmite, felt of his pulse, and forced himself to wait, to sit motionless, until his panic ebbed, and the beat of his racing heart became normal. He must think. Think calmly. There should be some means—

From far, far off came the hollow reverberating sound of a distant factory whistle—the five o'clock closing whistle of one of Malcolm Frain's industries.

Instantly Cathcart was on his feet again, stumbling, groping, at right angles to the source of the sound. Before it wholly died away he had reached the wall of the cave, and had turned and started to edge along the wall toward the sound.

The wall was jagged. Often huge stalagmites blocked his way, causing him to detour from the precious guiding wall. But always, after avoiding such an obstacle, he managed to find his way—half panicked—back to the wall again, and grope on.

And then finally dim daylight ahead! Gradually the light grew brighter as Cathcart's progress became more and more rapid, until suddenly the light paled and vanished, and jet blackness reigned once more.

Six o'clock!

Cathcart groped his way to the side of the cave again. But could he be sure that he had not become turned around? To his sense of direction it seemed certain that he had, that he was now headed back toward the interior of the cave. Every instinct counseled him to reverse; but he mastered his instinct, and kept on.

And then, just as he was about to falter, irresolute, a branch snapped in his face. He was in bushes. He was out of the cavern!

He found the clearing, stumbled across it, and groped about the woods on the further side, until his feet felt the trail.

A few minutes later he was in the open again, starless sky overhead, but with the twinkling lights of isolated farmhouses all about him, and far ahead a glow in the sky that indicated the headquarters city of the colony.

He reached the city, and at last the house of Herr Doktor Freundlich, without further event.

The genial Freundlich and his blonde sister had been worried for Cathcart, and received him with joy and relief.

"Lost in the woods," was all that Cathcart would say at first, but after he had eaten, and Emily Freundlich and the fluttery maid, Minna, had withdrawn, he told Dr. Freundlich what had happened.

THE two men were seated together in the privacy of the study.

"I cannot understand it," muttered Freundlich. "It is a door to which I find no key."

But Cathcart's attention had suddenly been attracted elsewhere. "Look, Doktor!" he exclaimed, his eyes riveted upon a little bug, half an inch long, scuttling across one corner of the desk; a tiny jointed insect with many legs, its body silver-colored.

"A silver-fish. So?" Then abruptly something gleamed in the pale eyes of Freundlich's round face. "Ach, yah! A silver-fish! The beast of the cave! The same! But why should Malcolm Frain breed a silver-fish one thousand times its natural size?"

"Dr. Freundlich," said Cathcart levelly. "That cave is not an accidental rift. It was planned. Beyond the intangible black curtain at its further end there lies something that may give us a clue to all this mystery. No wonder Donna Frain wanted the monster disposed of in secrecy. She was afraid that its accidental escape from whatever lies beyond that cave might give away the whole nature of her father's universe..." He jumped to his feet.

"My young friend," Freundlich replied, his pale eyes glowing. "We must go at once to that cave, with adequate lights, and explore it together. And we must take with us a phonograph to record those sounds that you heard."

Cathcart sat heavily down again. "I could not find that wood in the dark."

Freundlich shrugged his fat little shoulders. "And I too must wait for morning. We cannot obtain a recording phonograph at this hour of night."

Cathcart went to bed early, thoroughly tired out by his day's adventures.

Early next morning at the Frain laboratories, he and Dr. Freundlich requisitioned a phonograph—an ordinary one, inasmuch as there was none in the colony adapted to recording. But it was an easy matter for the two friends to modify a spare sound-box into one that would record rather than reproduce, and to fashion and groove some disks of soft wax. By working with feverish haste, they were able to complete their work before noon.

"And now," Freundlich announced, relaxing, "how about knocking off for the rest of the day and having a picnic? We can hire a government car."

"What!" Cathcart exclaimed. "Waste valuable time picnicking?"

"Well," said Freundlich, shrugging and beaming. "I rather thought that a certain clearing in a certain wood would be an ideal spot for lunch.

"A little cave-mouth hidden by the bough, a phonograph, some unscored disks, and thou beside me listening to the rumbling—"

"Okay. I catch on. But how will the authorities like our quitting work without permission?"

Freundlich replied, "I am sufficiently high in the organization, so that my time is my own."

Hiding the phonograph in the bottom of a large hamper of lunch, they set out in a Frain V-8 for the wood of the silver beast.

THEY were just unpacking their lunch in the clearing when down the trail came Sergeant Terro and a squad of soldiers.

"Ahhh…" Terro exclaimed, his black eyebrows lifting. "So it's you, Private Cathcart? I saw an auto headed in here, and hurried over to investigate. You're not, by any chance—?"

"Why, Sergeant…" Dr. Freundlich interrupted, looking up with an expression of complete innocence on his pudgy face. "This wood is not verboten, is it? Dr. Cathcart told me—"

"Cathcart!" Terra snapped. "You—"

Cathcart rushed over and seized the Sergeant by the arm. "Easy there!" he whispered. "Be careful what you say. Dr. Freundlich knows nothing⌐—doesn't even suspect anything. He asked me where I was yesterday, so I brought him here just to keep him from suspecting." Then raising his voice, ostensibly for the purpose of letting Freundlich hear, "Get away with you and leave us alone, or I'll put in a complaint to the Boss. This wood is not posted."

Terro winked, and a grin spread over his swarthy face. "I get you, pal," he said, as he withdrew with his troops.

Cathcart returned to his companion. "Weasel-Face trusts me as far as you can throw a bull by the tail," he reported, "which is considerably further than I trust him. He'll stick around, out of sight. We'll merely picnic."

So they merely picnicked. After eating, they dug a hole and buried their refuse. And with it they buried their recording apparatus. Then they returned to the city in their car.

At the laboratory that afternoon they found a black-uniformed Inspector awaiting them, restlessly pacing up and down.

"Where have you been?" the man snapped. "There is immediate need of you. One of the prisoners who has been running road-levels near here has escaped. Of course, we'll catch him and punish him, for no one can flout the Boss with impunity. But in the meantime this particular road-gang is being held up. The foreman suggested that perhaps one of you scientists might possibly be practical enough to be able to run a surveyor's level. Can you?"

"Why, certainly," Freundlich replied with surprising alacrity. "We both can. We'll be glad to."

"Only one is needed," the Inspector snapped.

"Ah, my friend," Freundlich apologized. "We scientists

would operate the instrument slightly differently from a civil engineer—would take notes in our own way—although the final results would be intelligible to your surveyors. So I am very much afraid, Sir, that you will have to put up with the two of us."

"All right! All right! Come along."

Dr. Freundlich turned to his assistant, and screwed up that side of his face furthest from the official into a laborious wink. Cathcart shook his head in perplexity.

A government car was waiting outside. Dr. Freundlich sat with the driver; Cathcart with the Inspector in the rear seat.

Apparently just to make conversation, Cathcart asked, "You say one of the road gang escaped?"

"Yes."

"Are such escapes frequent?"

"Altogether too much so, recently."

"But of course you'll catch them all eventually?"

"Certainly. Where could they go? They can't get out of the colony."

Cathcart laughed good-humoredly. "Of course not. And why should anyone want to leave? I like it here. Oh, by the way, who was the level-operator who escaped?"

"Fellow named Foley."

"Um."

The Inspector faced Cathcart, and eyed him sharply. "Know the fellow?" he snapped.

"Oh, yes," Cathcart replied airily. "He came down here in the same batch with me. Newspaper reporter, I believe. I never knew him on Earth." But to himself he thought, I wonder what Mickey is up to. Something harebrained, I'll bet.

THE road gang where they were to work was not far from the headquarters city. As Dr. Freundlich was introduced to the foreman and took over the leveling instrument, he said in a somewhat apologetic tone, "Mind if I and my young friend do a bit of practicing and checking before we start on the regular work? We are laboratory men, not surveyors, you know."

The foreman nodded his assent, and Freundlich and Cathcart took the instrument off onto a side road.

"Fortunately, it's a Y-level, rather than a dumpy, and thus quicker to adjust," Dr. Freundlich announced to his colleague. "We've got to work fast."

"At what?"

"I'm going to find out definitely whether this world is flat or curved."

He set up the machine, took a few sights through it, and completed his adjustment. Then sent Cathcart far down the road with the rod. For half an hour they sighted, changed position, sighted, and computed.

Then Dr. Freundlich perplexedly announced. "Your young newspaper friend Mickey Foley had the right hunch. This earth is absolutely flat⌐—that is to say insofar as anything short of absolute laboratory precision can measure it. And how can anyone expect us to get laboratory precision with a Y-level on a country road?"

"No one does expect you even to try, Doctor," Cathcart laughed. "In fact, if anyone suspected you of trying, you'd be tried yourself—for treason to Malcolm Frain."

The rest of the afternoon, until the closing whistle, they devoted to legitimate road surveying. But that evening, under cover of darkness, they sneaked out to the wood where they had picnicked earlier that day. With them they carried two flashlights, plenty of spare batteries, and two empty briefcases. They went on foot, rather than by car, so as to avoid detection.

Arriving at the clearing without event, they dug up their recording phonograph and blank records, and carried them into the cave.

"I hope this gets us somewhere," Cathcart doubtfully remarked.

"It may be the clue, as old Omar says, 'Could you but find it—to the Treasure-house, and peradventure to the Master too.' "

"Meaning Boss Frain?"

"Yes, though I rather suspect that you had rather it led to Boss Frain's daughter. Eh, my young friend?"

"Donna means nothing to me," Cathcart muttered embarrassedly.

"Ah! So you call her 'Donna' do you? Well, as you would say, let's skip it. Come on…"

CATHCART was surprised to find how much more quickly he traversed the one-mile path amid the towering stalagmites this time. Soon they stood before the wavering curtain of impenetrable darkness at the inner end of the cave.

Dr. Freundlich gingerly approached first one side of the black mist and then the other, and each time ran his hands around the edge into the darkness. "A flat barrier wall, as at our end of the cave. Another pocket in space, like our colony. But this darkness puzzles me—doubtless some gas impenetrable to our octave of light."

He took from his pocket several vacuum bottles, held them through the wavering veil, removed the stopples and let them fill, then examined them by the light of his torch—their contents proved impervious to its light.

"Hmmm…" he remarked, replacing them in his pocket.

Far out above them came the mysterious rhythmic booming that Cathcart had heard before. They assembled their phonograph and recorded all their records. They then repacked their apparatus and thoughtfully threaded their way back through the cave.

"You know, Cathcart," ruminated Dr. Freundlich, "I've been thinking. Did you ever notice the electric lights used in this colony? These flashlights for example."

"No, not particularly. Why?"

"Neither did I particularly, either," Freundlich enigmatically replied. "But I'm going to, as soon as I get home. For I've an idea."

But not a word more would he say on the subject.

On emerging from the cave, they buried the phonograph, and carried the records back with them in their two briefcases. But, instead of going home, they went directly to the laboratories. Dr. Freundlich often worked there late at night without being questioned; and tonight, if questioned, he would have an added excuse—the interruption caused by the afternoon's surveying.

First he set about to analyze the gas from one of the electric bulbs, and discovered it to be an obscure mixture, theoretically impervious to any light except extreme ultraviolet several octaves above normal. "And yet it permits the passage of the light that we see. Hmm. Now I begin to wonder about the photographic plates that are used down here. I know that the emulsion is one of the Boss's secrets. Photographic plates and electric bulbs are both made in the Frain Optical Works, over at the other end of the colony. The factory is guarded with great secrecy, and even I, a Frain scientist, have never been permitted to enter it. Tomorrow I shall make me some photographic plates of my own."

"What do you have in mind?"

"Some old Roman philosopher once said, 'Never disclose your plans until after they have been carried out.'"

"What? Quoting someone other than Omar?"

"Now you run along and get some sleep. Tomorrow you can analyze these samples I took of that veil of darkness."

Most of the next day in the laboratories the two men worked in silence and at separate benches.

Finally Cathcart announced, "This black stuff seems to react as ordinary air. Nothing else in it. I can't understand."

"Perhaps we shall know more tonight," Freundlich enigmatically replied.

That evening they again set out for the cave, with more blank records and Dr. Freundlich's camera; and, while Cathcart recorded the mysterious rumbling sounds, the doctor snapped plate after plate at the pulsating black void.

On their return to town, Freundlich insisted on their going to bed; but the next morning when they reached the laboratory he confessed to Cathcart that he himself had spent the balance of the night developing his plates. "And look what they show!" he exclaimed with suppressed excitement.

CHAPTER SIX
Donna in Danger

MOST of the plates were blurred, and some disclosed merely a series of dark pillars of various shapes and sizes, but on one plate there were dimly discernible two shadowy human figures, apparently seated on chairs, and distorted as though by being photographed by a camera on the floor.

"Giants," Freundlich announced in calm enough tones, though the pale blue eyes behind his thick lenses were flashing. "Giants about a mile high, so I deduce from the angle at which I took this picture, and from the degree of distortion of the various parts of the giant figures. But my telephoto lens was not set for quite a sufficient distance. We must go again tonight. Meanwhile let us develop our phonograph records."

They spent the rest of the day in coating their wax blanks with graphite, electroplating a negative film of metal on them, backing these metal films with cement, and then casting positive reproducing records from the moulds.

At supper Emily Freundlich informed them that the capital was seething. Wholesale escapes of road gang prisoners had occurred, troops were now scouring the colony in search of the fugitives, and a stop had been put temporarily to the shipment of further colonists from the Earth. But Dr. Freundlich and Robert Cathcart were too excited by their discovery of the world of the giants, to be affected by her agitation, or even to grasp fully the purport of what she was saying.

That evening they again set forth for the cave, this time carrying merely the camera and a large supply of plates.

As they walked along together, Dr. Freundlich asked, "Do you realize what those photographs prove?"

"That one of the cells of this cockeyed universe of Malcolm Frain is inhabited by giants? Anything more?"

"Yes. That the air of that cell is normal air, and that our air here is so peculiarly constituted as to be impervious to light within the range of human vision."

"You mean just the opposite, don't you?"

"No, I don't. That picture of the giants was taken on plates sensitive to normal light. I have reason to believe that our light here is four or five octaves into the ultra-violet."

"But how can we see it then? And why doesn't it kill us?"

"It actually was deadly to the huge silver-fish from the giant world. In my opinion, light killed him. But the status-changing machine, which brought us here, has probably changed our physical characteristics in some way so that we can see only ultraviolet rays, and so that those rays are harmless to us."

"But why?"

"As Omar says, 'That is the door to which I found no key.' "

They walked in silence the rest of the way. Having arrived at the cave in the wood, they entered it as before.

But only a short distance in, they found the way blocked by a pool of water on the floor, and beyond that a solid wall of damp rough stone!

"It looks to me," Dr. Freundlich remarked, "as though our giant friends had plastered up this little crack at the base of the wall of their world, so as to keep their little silver-fishes from escaping into our world."

"Considerate of them, I'm sure! Well, what do we do now?"

"Nothing, my young friend, except to return home and think. We have plenty to think about."

THE next morning, long before the time for the customary rising whistle, they were awakened by bugle notes, an unusual occurrence. Troops were marching in the streets. Officers were knocking on the doors, distributing handbills that proclaimed martial law throughout the colony and called all able-bodied men to the colors.

Wrapped up in the official notice was a crudely printed unofficial one, which read:

FREEMEN ARISE!

Cast off your shackles and defy Malcolm Frain. He dare not retaliate, for we hold his daughter Donna as a hostage. If enough of us revolt, we can compel the Boss to send us all back to the Earth where we belong. Further particulars will be published later. Pass this flyer on to a friend.

Down with Boss Frain!

THE POPULISTS.

Cathcart's jaw dropped and his eyes widened as he read it. Donna Frain kidnapped! Undoubtedly by that unprincipled scoundrel, Terro!

Frantically he slipped into some clothes and was about to rush to Headquarters with the handbill, when Dr. Freundlich stopped him, saying, "You go to the barracks and report for duty, or you'll get into trouble. Let me take this flyer to the authorities."

At the barracks Cathcart found a milling throng of excited civilians being issued uniforms and equipment. Everything was in confusion, officers shouting orders, and no one paying very much attention.

Someone thrust another handbill at Cathcart—an appeal to the soldiery to kill their officers and join the revolution. He hastened to an Inspector and handed over the paper. He had been bit once before by being caught with Populist literature in his possession, and didn't intend to be caught that way again.

Even this time he was immediately taken into custody and held for questioning. The whole Administration seemed to be in a panic.

Cathcart easily convinced his inquisitors that he knew nothing of the source of the circular. And furthermore he made a valuable contribution to the situation; for when they had finished interrogating him, he in turn asked a question, "Has anyone seen Sergeant Terro?"

No—no one had. So Cathcart told them that he knew of the man; of his treasonable utterances on Earth the day of their departure for this colony; of the fact that it had been Terro who had slipped him the Populist literature that had been found in his pocket the day of his arrival, and of Terro's several subversive statements to him since. But Cathcart still obeyed Donna Frain's orders to keep quiet about the giant insect in the wood.

"Why did you not report Terro's treason at once to the authorities?" the Inspector asked him.

Cathcart shrugged his broad shoulders. "Who would have believed me? Terro stood fairly high with the Administration. He was personal bodyguard to Donna—I mean, to Inspector Frain. Why should I stick my neck out? But I did continue to observe him whenever I was off duty. Dr. Freundlich will—"

He was about to say that Freundlich would confirm his story about asking time off to spy upon Putorius Terro; but suddenly he realized that this would implicate Dr. Freundlich. So he finished lamely, "He will confirm that I have asked for a lot of time off recently."

The investigators were too perturbed to notice his hesitation. The Inspector in charge merely snapped, "The failure to report this information will go against your record, Cathcart. But you have really given us a valuable lead. Besides we need every available man. So for the present you will not be arrested. Go join your squad."

CATHCART saluted and withdrew. He was loaded onto a truck with some other soldiers, and driven off across the plains.

Gradually order was made out of all the chaos, and a systematic plan was evolved. Cordons of soldiers, within fingertip distance of each other, swept through the entire colony. Every house and thicket was searched. Every citizen was bundled in to the nearest Registry, was checked against his card-record there, and was ordered under possible penalty of death not to leave a certain circumscribed area.

For about a week this kept on, until every square foot of the 1500 square miles of the colony had been scoured. More than a thousand men and their families were reported missing, and not a trace of them nor of Donna Frain and Putorius Terro could be found.

It was inexplicable! As many people as that just couldn't possibly vanish into thin air, especially in a completely hermetically sealed world such as this colony of Malcolm Frain's.

Of course the cave of the silver beast was discovered during the search. Or rather, it was discovered as the result of information obtained from one of the guards whom Terro and Donna had posted around the wood that day. This man reported the episode to the authorities as soon as the inquiries about Terro began. A guard was again posted, and the wood was scoured by specially selected Regular Army troops, with the result that when the ordinary searchers reached the place, the mouth of the cave had been sealed up and was passed almost unnoticed.

At the end of a fruitless week, the militia was dismissed and told to return to their homes. Cathcart trudged wearily back to the house of the Freundlichs, thoroughly discouraged. What could have become of the flaming Donna? The diabolical cleverness of his rival, Terro, intrigued and maddened him.

But there was one consolation: if Donna should ever escape or be rescued from her imprisonment, she certainly would have no further use for her captor. But then a doubt assailed Cathcart. What if Donna had gone willingly, and was a party to all this? But no, she could never be disloyal to her father. Still, women sometimes do strange things when infatuated.

DR. FREUNDLICH eagerly greeted him. "My young friend," he exclaimed, "I have made great progress in my experiments to determine the nature of this universe. Come, you must see."

Cathcart slumped into a chair, waved Freundlich away with one hand, and let his head fall dejectedly into the other. "Take it away, doctor," he groaned. "I don't care where we are, or what this universe is. All that want to know is what has become of Donna Frain."

"So do we all of us—all who are loyal to the Boss's daughter," Freundlich replied in a kindly voice. "And especially do I sympathize with your own deep personal interest in the subject. But listen, my young friend. Do you not realize that the nature of this universe may have an important bearing on the Fraulein's fate?"

Cathcart raised a haggard face. Then his eyes lit up, and he pulled himself erect. "Okay, Doc. You win. I'll listen to anything that has the slightest chance of helping to find the girl I love."

"So..." whistled Freundlich. "So you love her, eh? I have thought as much for some time. Come into my study."

There, seated in a comfortable stuffed leather chair, and soothed by a glass of his host's synthetic wine, Cathcart prepared to listen.

"First, my young friend, I have given up all attempt to measure the curvature of this world, although I do not subscribe to the theory that it is flat. If, as I suspect, its curvature is of the nature of seven one-millionths of an inch to a mile, it cannot be measured without the use of more delicate apparatus than I have available, and the spanning of a distance which would involve too much public exposure."

"I thought you said you had discovered something, not nothing," Cathcart dejectedly interjected.

"Ah, but I have truly discovered something—quite a great deal, in fact. First I have definitely proved that we are not on the Earth—as we know it. But this is only one of my experiments. Let us take a hypothesis, and proceed toward its verification or disproof."

"And what is that hypothesis?"

"That you and I, and all the rest of the people of this colony, are only seven hundredths of an inch tall. From Earth's Center is a long, long way by that scale. Hence no curvature."

"What...?" Cathcart sat suddenly erect. "Why that sounds completely absurd. Are you serious, Dr. Freundlich?"

"I am emphatically serious." The little man beamed at him from behind his thick glasses.

"But what is the evidence for your theory?"

"I thought you were a scientist, Dr. Cathcart. A true scientist needs no evidence in support of an hypothesis. Sufficient is it that no evidence conflicts with it. If we are only seven hundredths of an inch tall, this would account for there being no observable curvature of the Earth, and for the barometer not leveling off at thirty inches."

"Pretty slim," Cathcart said.

"Well, it would explain the nature of this room in which we find ourselves."

"You mean your study."

"No, I mean this whole thirty-nine-¬mile-square colony. Maybe this colony is the two-hundred-foot-square room in Malcolm Frain's warehouse, to which you carted the laboratory-treated silt several months ago. Maybe our coarse soil is that fine silt. Maybe the status¬-changing machine, which brought us here, is a size-reducer. Maybe—"

"HOLD on!" Cathcart interrupted. "If we are only one one-thousandth our natural size, the acceleration of gravity would be 32,160 feet per second per second, instead of only 32.16. Our weight would be unbearable."

"Unbearable nothing! Our mass would be reduced to one billionth of its Earth value, and the combined effect of mass and acceleration and reduction in height, would make our weight appear to be one one-thousandth of what it should. Too light, rather than too heavy. And anyway, I've measured g; it's normal."

"I have a theory," Cathcart asserted, warming up to the subject. "Suppose that our time-sense has been changed, too, so that a second of real time seems like thirty-two seconds to us; then, if our height has been reduced to 1/1024 of normal—"

"But why those figures?"

"Because of the thirty-two day month down here. May it not be that each day on Earth is a month in this colony. That would account for all the time-discrepancy, which we have observed. You've been here five years, while two months have elapsed on Earth. Terro left the Earth only a few hours ahead of me, and yet arrived here four days ahead."

Dr. Freundlich's pudgy face suddenly lit up. "Thirty-two times, exactly!" he exclaimed. "The Foucault pendulum! It rotates 28 minutes of arc per hour, exactly one thirty-second of what it should!"

Cathcart continued, "And, with time sped up to this extent, light would appear shifted five octaves into infra-red. In order for light to seem normal to us, Boss Frain must be flooding this warehouse with ultra-violet light, five octaves above visibility. But ordinary air is impervious to light as ultra as that, and such light would be lethal; so the Boss has probably status-changed the air of this miniature world of his, so as to pass the light; and the change in our own size-status is probably protective in some way. But look what it did to the silver-fish!"

"My experiment with the photographic plates checks with this," said Freundlich. But he was frowning now, and Cathcart could see that something was puzzling or worrying the older scientist.

Just as Cathcart was about to inquire, sounds of cheering outside interrupted him. The two men rushed to the front door, and flung it open. A parade of soldiers was marching past in the brightly-lighted street. In their midst rode Boss Frain himself, in the trim black uniform of the Frain Guards, seated regally on a black horse, receiving the plaudits of the multitude. Quite evidently he had visited this world of his to take personal command of the operations against the Populists, and of the search for his missing daughter.

Somehow the presence of this great man was very comforting and reassuring to Robert Cathcart. He had never seen the Boss before. Bushy browed, keen-eyed, hawk-nosed, and firm jawed, sitting erect upon his charger, Boss Frain radiated energy and confidence. With him in charge, Donna would surely be found. Spontaneously Cathcart let out a cheer, and the god of his destinies turned and smiled in his direction in acknowledgment of the greeting. Then the procession passed on.

AS Cathcart and Freundlich returned to the study, the latter dryly observed, "So you can see, my young friend, from the way in which you yourself reacted just now, the personal magnetism that enabled Malcolm Frain to rise to the dominating position that he occupies. And yet, if our theories are correct, that man Frain has arrogated to himself the right to hold in the hollow of his hand all of us who dwell in this miniature world that he has created. A mere flip of a switch could plunge us in darkness forever.

A crack in the walls could let in ordinary air through which we could not see, even by artificial illumination. A larger crack would let in outside light, infrared and searing to our status-changed sensibilities. Suppose he were to shut off the rain, and deprive us of water. Or leave it on, and flood us out."

Cathcart shuddered. "Let's hope our theories are wrong!" he fervently exclaimed.

"Perhaps they are, for I have just thought of one fact that may upset our entire hypothesis. Muscular strength, all other things being equal, varies with the cross-section of the muscle. With weight reduced one billionth, and strength reduced only one millionth, a man here should be a thousand times as strong as on Earth."

"Let's pass that over for the moment," Cathcart suggested. "Why not measure the velocity of light?"

Freundlich smiled. "You forget relativity. The velocity of light is independent of the observer; it is an absolute quantity."

But Cathcart persisted. "Independent of position or motion of the observer, yes. But not independent of either the size or the time-sense of the observer."

"I believe you have something there," Freundlich mused. "I shall start building a gear-wheel light-interrupter tomorrow."

The next day the detailed combing already given to every square foot of the colony was repeated under the watchful eyes of the Boss in person. The Boss rode everywhere among the searchers, on his black horse, encouraging them, urging them on. But it was no use. Not a single clue did they turn up. And a re-check of the populace developed the fact that several hundred more citizens had disappeared since the first combing.

Toward the end of the week, as Cathcart was patrolling one of the streets of Town 13, he saw Mickey Foley ducking into an alley. Here at last was a clue, which any other member of the Frain's army, not knowing Foley, would have missed. Silently Cathcart raced to the alley mouth. It was a dead-ender. Foley was running rapidly toward a fence at the further end.

Whipping out his revolver, Cathcart shouted, "Halt, Mickey, or I'll fire."

But, without pausing or glancing back, Foley vaulted over the fence. Cathcart fired. And suddenly everything went black.

For a moment, Cathcart thought that something had hit and stunned him; that someone had fired back, simultaneously with his own shot.

But no. There was no numbness, no dizziness. Everything was quite all right, except that he could not see. He groped to the side of a building and leaned against it. Far down the street in the jet darkness, isolated lights began to twinkle here and there. Then the window of a house across the road lit up, and he could see himself and his surroundings by the diffused radiance that poured out.

A clatter of hoofs, and Malcolm Frain dashed by, alone, unguarded, his eyes wide, his face ashen with fright.

Then the shades were pulled down, and once more Cathcart was in darkness.

At last the street lights came on, street by street. Cathcart ran to the end of the alley and peered over the fence—no sign of Mickey Foley. So he set out for local Headquarters to report.

But would anything be accomplished by reporting? The Authorities had proved quite impotent thus far. And somehow Cathcart had the same degree of instinctive confidence in the little Irish newspaper reporter that he had distrust of the swarthy Terro. Perhaps Mickey's presence among the revolutionaries would be a protection to Donna Frain. Cathcart must do nothing to deprive her of that protection. So he turned around and retraced his steps to his beat. And then he suddenly noticed that it was broad daylight again.

WHEN he was relieved of his post, and returned to local Headquarters, Malcolm Frain was there, his poise somewhat recovered, but his eyes furtive and hunted. The others, not having seen what Cathcart had seen, did not appear to notice.

The brief spell of darkness was explained as having been an eclipse. But how could an eclipse occur in a world that has no sun? While Cathcart and Boss Frain were still there, several of the patrols brought in copies of a new Populist manifesto, this time boldly signed by Terro's name, demanding the immediate recall of all troops, under penalty of death to Donna Frain; but promising to spare her life if the Boss obeyed. And a dated letter, written in Donna's unmistakable handwriting, had been found in a mailbox, declaring that she still lived, but that she was refusing, even under threat of torture, to beg her father to save her.

Foolish bravery! Her letter was just as effective without the plea.

Boss Frain read the flyer, and then his daughter's letter, and then the flyer again. His grizzled jaw was set and grim, but there was a trace of moisture in his steely eye.

He loved his daughter more than he loved his power. But even in defeat he was firm, decisive.

"Call off the troops!" he commanded. "And announce that I have done so. But announce also that if any harm comes to my daughter, every man, woman and child in this colony will be put to a horrible death."

This concluding threat chilled in Cathcart the sympathetic warmth that he was beginning to feel for Donna's father. And yet would not he himself be willing to deal the same to anyone who injured her?

He returned to Headquarters City not quite as glumly as at the end of the former search. For now he knew that Donna was still alive, and his glimpse of Mickey Foley was strong evidence to him that the whole band of conspirators was still in some quite tangible locality within this cellular world.

But where? Suddenly the solution dawned on him. A cave! Another cave, like the one from which had come the silver beast. Such a cave could easily house several thousand persons.

Accordingly, he resolved that as soon as his military patrol was dismissed, he would lay the idea before the Boss in person; it was too good of a hunch to waste upon stupid subordinates. Besides, the suggestion might boost his stock with Donna's father. First, however, he would broach his theory to Dr. Freundlich, and ask Freundlich's advice and influence for securing an audience with Malcolm Frain.

But the troops were not dismissed immediately upon their arrival, for first an official circular had to be distributed from house to house, explaining that an "eclipse" was as normal and natural an occurrence here as on Earth. So it was late evening when Cathcart, still in uniform, finally reached the house of his patron; but Dr. Freundlich was still up.

THE genial little man waited patiently, though with

suppressed excitement, while Cathcart announced his theory as to the hiding-place of the Populists, and recounted the events of the week. Then Freundlich, his pale eyes flashing, sprung his own news.

"I have measured the speed of light. It is thirty-two times what it should be, thus confirming our hypothesis. Even the question of the muscular strength is solved, for I have found in our library an obscure paper by the great Carey of Marquette, in which he expresses doubt that muscular strength varies as the square of its dimensions—in fact, he even hints that it may possibly vary as the cube. This hidden universe of Malcolm Frain's—which is nothing but a warehouse stall—confirms Carey's guess."

"Then it is true that Boss Frain holds us in the hollow of his hand," Cathcart exclaimed softly, bleak horror in his eyes. "We are mere tiny insects crawling in the silt of a warehouse floor..."

Dr. Freundlich nodded solemnly. "And nothing can be done about it. But I have a still greater surprise for you. Come to my laboratory."

At the laboratory, Freundlich put a record on a phonograph, wound up the machine, and placed the needle in the groove. From the sound-box there came a slow, almost musical, deep rumble, rising and falling in uneven waves.

"The noise from behind the black curtain in the cave of the silver beast," Cathcart commented. "But what of it?"

The rotund face of Dr. Freundlich beamed impishly. "And now I will speed it up thirty-two times," He made an adjustment and replayed the record. "Listen..."

Out of the sound-box came the unmistakable voice of Malcolm Frain, saying: "And so, Mr. Secretary, this is my ultimatum to America. You and I and the President are among the few who realize that War is about to break. America is not ready. I alone can make her ready. I have secret means whereby I can speed up the manufacture of munitions and the training of troops thirty-¬two times the normal rate. Think of it! A month's training for raw recruits in a single day. It may seem impossible to you, Mr. Secretary, but you will have to believe me, for the sake of America. However, I am not patriotic; I am a hardheaded businessman; and my price is—" A scraping sound, and the record ended.

"Isn't that perfect?" Freundlich exulted. "Even to the mention of the mystic number, 32!"

"What interests me more than that," said Cathcart soberly, "is the impending fate of America, and the price that the Boss is to exact to save her."

"I thought," Freundlich maliciously replied, "that it was another 'she,' whom you were anxious to save."

"Donna… How could I have forgotten her even for an instant? I must see her father at once."

But his genial host held up a restraining hand. "Wait," he said. "Listen to the remaining phonograph records, so that you may know the manner of man with whom you have to deal."

SO the rest of the records were played. They revealed an amazing situation. By piecing together scraps of recorded conversation, the two scientists were able to figure out that "Mr. Secretary" was the Secretary of War of the United States, that he had cast dignity aside and had come to beg the great Industrialist to save America, and that Frain's price for this service was that he be appointed Secretary of State, and that the President and Vice President both resign.

"A man with such a profound lack of patriotism and such vaulting ambition," Freundlich grimly commented, "would stoop to anything, even to the sacrifice of his own daughter."

"I doubt that," Cathcart defended. "Remember please that Frain withdrew the troops when she was threatened. I was with him at the time, and saw his face—it reflected a struggle between love of Donna and love of power. And I believe love of Donna won out."

"Well, anyway, this 'colony,' as he calls it, is a mere toy of his. Suppose he tires of it, what then? Remember the 'eclipse?' Undoubtedly a mere instant's stoppage of the electric current that lights this miniature world. Man, do you realize that Malcolm Frain, by a mere flip of a switch, could snuff us all out? If anything happens to his daughter that's what he'll do—in revenge. Or suppose some subordinate electrician blunders for a mere minute of Earth time—a half-hour of our time down here. Or suppose that something should happen to Boss Frain, and leave persons in charge who don't understand the nature of this cockeyed universe of his...?"

Cathcart soberly replied, "My mind tells me that you are right, but I can't quite sense it. I can't realize that it's so."

"If you ever do realize it, my young friend, remember to hang onto yourself; for it will take a great effort of your will not to go stark raving mad. Remember Malcolm Frain's terror¬-stricken flight during the 'eclipse.' He realized it then."

The ringing of the telephone interrupted them. It was the maid Minna, all aflutter, to tell them that the Boss was at the house with an armed guard, demanding that they return immediately.

They did so, with considerable trepidation.

MALCOLM FRAIN was pacing up and down the living room in his black uniform with the insignia of a Field Marshal. On his face was the look of an impatient man, a man not used to waiting too long. An insignia one grade higher than any American—even George Washington—had ever worn.

"Where have you two been?" he demanded accusingly, as they entered.

"Why—why—" Freundlich stammered, "we have been conducting a number of experiments—in the laboratory, Herr Boss."

"Scientific experiments at a time like this?" snapped Frain. "It was such an attitude that cost Archimedes his life at the fall of Carthage."

"But Carthage is not going to fall this time, Sir," Cathcart cut in.

Malcolm Frain turned deep-set eyes set upon him. "A bold young man," he commented approvingly. "I wish a word alone with you."

Dr. Freundlich interposed, "There is a garden behind the house, Excellency, with a high wall about it."

"Lead us there, and then leave us," Frain peremptorily commanded.

In the garden, Frain eyed Cathcart searchingly for a moment by the dim light that filtered in from the glare of the surrounding city. "I am told that you are loyal," he stated.

"I admire your great accomplishments," Cathcart replied. He hesitated. "I—I would not like any harm to come to your daughter."

"And you know something about where Terro has hidden her?" Frain shrewdly surmised. "You alone of all of us have had the insight to see through Terro from the very beginning. Also you have shown an ability to hold your tongue; the episode of the silver-f—the silver beast proves that."

Cathcart decided to make a bold play. "Excellency," he replied, "I don't wish to incur your wrath, but I know the nature of this hidden universe of yours. I know that it is merely a room two hundred feet square in one of your New Jersey warehouses. I know that all us colonists are at your mercy. I know—"

"What! You know all this, and are still loyal? You know all this, and still have not disclosed it to your fellow colonists? Why?"

"Because the knowledge of it would drive men mad. I saw the expression on your face when you were fleeing from the 'eclipse.' "

Frain stiffened. "Men have died for seeing less than that," he rasped. "Remember that you are no longer in a free country, Cathcart. I am autocrat here. Well, go on."

"Your Excellency, realizing all this, I hoped that by serving you with unswerving loyalty, I could finally get close enough to you—"

Frain fell back a step, and his hand went instinctively to his hip.

But Cathcart spread his arms wide to show that he was unarmed, and hurriedly continued, "—so as to persuade you to undo all this, and lead us back to the safety of the real world. That is to say, after first using this colony as the means to thwart the threatened invasion of America."

"What?" Frain gasped. "You know of that, too? How is that possible? How?"

"I am a scientist," Cathcart replied.

Boss Frain was smiling now, his momentary surprise

ended. "Suppose I were to tell you that your scientific theories are absurd and unfounded? Suppose I were to command you to forget them?"

"I should refuse to either believe or obey you."

"Cathcart! You have gone too far..."

"Boss Frain," Cathcart boldly replied, "let's cut out the sparring. You have the power to kill me, if you wish. You can snuff out this whole colony. I know it. But, my lord, man, we both want to find Donna. Let's get going!"

Frain tried to keep his face grim, but it broke into an approving smile. "Young man...I like you," he said softly. "Well...what do you suggest?"

"I have a theory as to where the Populists are holding your daughter."

The crack of a pistol resounded through the quiet garden!

"He got me!" cried Frain, collapsing to the ground with a gurgling groan.

Something thudded onto the patch beside them. An automatic! Cathcart scooped it up.

A dark form was scaling the garden wall, silhouetted against the diffused glare of the city. Cathcart leveled the weapon, and squeezed the trigger. But no shot came.

Unloaded! He might have known.

He bent over the fallen Boss. The shouts of approaching guards could be heard within the house.

This, then, was the end. Alone with the Boss. The Boss murdered. And Cathcart's fingerprints on the butt of the murder weapon!

CHAPTER SEVEN
Flight

THE evidence would be conclusive that Cathcart had killed Boss Frain. And yet his first impulse was not to flee; but rather to stay, in the hope that the father of the girl he loved was not dead.

Yet how unnecessary! The body would be discovered in a few seconds, and Dr. Freundlich and the Boss's retainers would do whatever could be done for the stricken man. So Cathcart thrust the empty pistol into one of his side pockets and scrambled lithely over the garden wall, landing in a dimly lit alley.

No sign anywhere of the assassin. Cathcart dogtrotted silently to one end of the alley, and peered out. Plenty of people in the street, many of the men being dressed in the black Frain uniform like himself, Cathcart mingled with the throng, and walked slowly along, his mind in a daze.

Gradually his senses cleared, and there came to him a realization of the hopelessness of his predicament. Not his own personal predicament as the putative slayer of the Boss, but rather his predicament in common with all these other poor souls trapped in this hidden universe, which really was merely a room in a New Jersey warehouse. Malcolm Frain himself had admitted as much by his silence in the face of Cathcart's statements.

And, now that Frain was dead, now that his daughter and sole heir was a prisoner of revolutionaries within this same trap, what assurance was there that the elaborate man-made mechanism, which supported life within this artificial world, would continue to function!

Cathcart felt a sudden urge to run, to shriek, to seek the barrier wall and beat his fists upon it. But a recollection of the words of kindly old Freundlich stayed him. What had the roly-poly little scientist said? "If you ever reach a full realization of the nature of this miniature world that Malcolm Frain has created hang onto yourself; for it will take a great effort of will not to go stark raving mad."

Cathcart squared his shoulders and drew in a deep breath. He could face the realization. And, from now on, his problem transcended saving his own neck from an undeserved charge of murder. It even went beyond rescuing Donna Frain for her own sweet sake. He must rescue her for the more important purpose of enabling her to take over her father's control of the destinies of these thousands of poor human mites crawling microscopically in the fine silt spread upon a warehouse floor.

An official car was drawn up beside the curb. Cathcart thanked his stars that the Frain V-8s of this starless world had no locks, since theft was believed impossible here. In an instant Cathcart was in the car, headed for the outskirts of the city, selecting and traversing a little-traveled route. Still no signs of pursuit.

But when he reached the district line, he understood. Instead of a hue and cry, the authorities had merely blocked the exits. A black and white striped gate was down, and in the middle of the road stood a sentry with automatic pistol held at the alert.

CATHCART drew to a stop, and leaned out of the car window. "Private Robert Jones, on an official errand for the Boss," he announced.

"The Boss is dead," the sentinel grimly replied.

"My God, no!" Cathcart exclaimed, his eyes widening and his jaw dropping with well-simulated astonishment. "Why, he gave me this dispatch in person not half an hour ago at the house of Professor Freundlich! How did it happen?"

"Assassinated by a guy named Cathcart. Orders are to let no one leave the city."

So the supposed crime was known already? Of course, it would be. Yet somehow the actuality was more staggering than the expectation had been.

Cathcart shuddered. Then pulled himself together. "But, man, this dispatch must go through. The Boss's death makes it all the more important. Look, I'll show you my pass."

He got out of the car, and started fumbling in the pockets of his military blouse. The guard drew nearer, expectantly, and lowered his gun. Instantly out shot Cathcart's fist, straight to the point of the man's jaw. As the fellow crashed to the ground, Cathcart leaped back into the car, stepped on the gas, crashed through the striped gate, and was off down the road toward open country.

But he had won only a slight respite. The guard would soon be found, and then—pursuit!

About five miles out, and five miles short of the next town, he saw the tail lights of another car ahead. As he passed it, he noted that it too was official. Pulling to a stop a short distance beyond it, he drew his car across the narrow road, blocking it, honked several times, got out, and held up his hand, bathed in the headlights of the other car.

It stopped. Its occupant got out and approached him. An Inspector of about his own size and build.

Cathcart saluted. "Sorry to stop you, Sir, but I'm on special patrol, to inform all Inspectors who haven't been reached by radio or telephone, that the Boss has been murdered and that they are to be on the lookout for his assassin."

The Inspector was eyeing him suspiciously. "My car is equipped with short-wave," he crisply replied. "I know all about it, and am on the same mission myself."

"Then stick 'em up, Sir," gritted Cathcart, reaching in his pocket for his empty gun.

Up slowly into the air went the officer's hands. Cathcart stepped forward as though to search him, but instead clouted him over the head with the barrel of his gun. The man collapsed without a sound to the pavement.

Rapidly Cathcart dragged the inert form into a nearby field, ran his own car off the road, knocking down a fence to make it look like an accident, and switched off the lights. Then he pulled loose some wires, changed blouse and cap and gun with the Inspector, and propped the body up behind the wheel.

AS HE continued on his way in the Inspector's car, he commented grimly to himself, "If they discover the car before the Inspector comes to, it'll be a clear case accidentally running off the road. If he comes to finds he can't start the car, and staggers into some nearby town or farmhouse, no one will believe his story. In either case, he'll be arrested for being me, and in the meantime I have all the necessary papers to identify me as Inspector Talbot. And a short-wave radio to keep track of the pursuit. What a break!"

His identification papers got him by the next two barriers. But Cathcart began to wonder how long he could succeed with this impersonation. So finally on the outskirts of Town 13, which he had picked as his destination, he parked the car and reconnoitered.

The open lighted window of a farmhouse attracted his attention. He crept up to it and peered in. It was a bedroom, vacant for the moment. Beyond it he could hear the sounds of a man singing and splashing in a bathtub. On a chair by the window was a suit of clothes.

Cathcart reached in and took the clothes. Hastily slipping into them behind the barn, he threw his uniform into the manure pit, and resumed his car. By the car's dome-light, he inspected the contents of the pockets of the purloined suit, and to his joy found a pass, dated that very day, entitling Thomas Thistle to enter and leave Town 13. So running the Inspector's car into a side road he switched off the headlights removed and hid the distributor, and set out on foot the remaining half mile or so to the town.

His pass got him into town all right. But now what? As he was walking thoughtfully along the almost deserted streets, trying to recall the exact locality where he had seen Mickey Foley, a Corporal in uniform accosted him. "Pretty late to be on the streets, Colonist. Let's see your pass."

Cathcart pulled it out and handed it over. The soldier tilted it to read it by the light of a nearby streetlamp, then wheeled around with, "You're not Thistle! I know the man. Who are you?"

"Oh, I must have Tom's pass by mistake. That's too bad. You see I'm visiting Tom, and—" Out shot his fist, spilling the Corporal into the gutter.

But the blow was ill aimed. The soldier was up in an instant, his automatic clutched in his hand. "Halt, or I fire!" he cried.

Cathcart fled.

A shot rang out behind him. Another, and another. He dodged down an alley.

But it was the same dead-end alley into which he had formerly chased Mickey Foley or another one much like it. Over the fence at the end went Cathcart, just as Foley had done that other time. Cathcart groped his way across a yard in the darkness, scaled a fence at the further side, and found himself another alley. The black form of the soldier appeared on the top of the wall, silhouetted dimly against the sky. Cathcart reached into his pocket for the Inspector's gun, and then realized that he had left it in the Inspector's clothes, which he had heaved into the manure-pit. So he flattened himself into a dark doorway. The pursuing soldier dropped from the wall, and trotted by.

Cathcart heaved a sigh of relief, lost his balance slightly, and leaned against the door for support. But the door swung open, and he sprawled into a brightly-lighted room. He blinked, sprang to his feet, and looked into the muzzle of a revolver.

Behind it was the grinning freckled face of the little Irish tabloid reporter.

"Well, if it isn't the assassin in person!" Foley exclaimed, lowering the gun and closing the door. "You're one of us now, whether you like it or not. Wouldn't this make the front page! But we must be quick about it. This way!"

HE snapped off the lights, and led Cathcart groping through several rooms and down some stairs, then turned on a single dim light. They were in a cellar room with tiled walls, Foley pressed on one of the tiles, and a small section of the wall swung open, disclosing a long low dirt tunnel. Into this they crawled, closing the smoothly hinged wall-section behind them.

"Well, Cathcart," said Foley, as they crawled along, "how come you killed the Boss?"

"It's a long story, and I think I'd better save it for Mr. Terro."

"Oho! So you know where I'm taking you?"

"Naturally. This is where I was heading for. Lucky thing your door was open."

"Damn careless of me I'd say. You might have been a cop. Please don't tell our Leader that you got in without giving the countersign."

"I won't," Cathcart promised, grinning to himself in the dark.

The tunnel ended against a smooth face of hard rock, and turned sharp to the left. Dim light could be seen ahead. As they crawled nearer, this light was disclosed as coming from a narrow crack in the wall to their right.

Through this crack they squeezed, and stood erect in a cavern just like the lair of the silver beast. This then was the hideout of the Populist revolutionaries; Cathcart had been correct in his guess.

A heavily armed squad of determined-looking men in civilian clothes stopped them just inside the cave, and expressed great surprise and joy when informed as to the identity of the newcomer. "Our Leader will certainly be glad!" they exclaimed.

But Cathcart wondered whether Terro would be glad to see him; and if so, glad for what reason and what purpose.

"So long, Bob. Wish you luck with us," said Foley, turning back.

"So long, Mickey. I'll give you the story exclusive for your paper some day, if we ever get out of here."

Then one of the guards led Cathcart away, down the cavern.

This crack in the barrier-wall was larger than it had been in the cave that he and Dr. Freundlich had explored. Along one side stood crude houses of rough board. Additional houses were in the process of construction. Water ¬pipes and a sewer-main lay along the floor of the cavern, and the whole place was well lighted. Fortunately for the conspirators, neither water nor electricity were metered in the Frain colony, and so the diversion would never be noticed or even traced to here.

Finally Cathcart reached a house more pretentious than the others and was led inside. A crude printing press was working. There were file-cabinets along the wall and a number of clerks at desks. Two soldiers, incongruously clad in the Frain uniform, although at war with Frain, stood one on each side of a closed door. One of them stepped inside, reported, and then ushered Cathcart in.

At a desk facing the entrance, sat Putorious Terro, swarthy, oily, and self-assured. He, too, wore the black uniform of the government against which he was rebelling, and on each shoulder were the five stars of a Field Marshal.

CATHCART'S gray eyes narrowed, and he was about to remark that his former truck-driver associate had certainly come up in the world; but he restrained himself and saluted.

"Well, Cathcart," said Terro, his closely set eyes boring into the man who stood in front of him, "we meet again. So you have at last taken my advice to join our cause? But perhaps you have come too late."

"I hope not," Cathcart replied, grinning quizzically.

Terro evidently misinterpreted the grin as an attempt to be ingratiating, and the remark as an expression of hope that the lateness of Cathcart's eleventh hour conversion would not be held against him. "What have you got to prove that you are on the up and up with us? The killing of the Boss?"

"No," said Cathcart, his grey eyes narrowing. "But rather a frank admission that I am entitled to no credit whatever for his death."

Terro raised his bushy black eyebrows. "Your frankness surprises me. Who did bump off the Boss?"

"I thought you knew."

"Oh! Then your frankness doesn't surprise me one bit. I sent several guys to do the 'dirty work,' but none of them have reported back yet, so I was afraid that you'd beaten them to it. So Frain's really croaked?"

"I was alone with him when he died. That's why I'm getting both the credit and the blame for it."

"Wish I could be sure you're not stringing me along. Maybe your whole yarn is some kind of frame-up. You got here too damned easy for a guy who's on the lam. And just how did you find our hangout?"

"I just happened to—" But no, Cathcart thought, he mustn't betray Foley's carelessness in leaving that door unlocked. "I just happened to be running away from a soldier. I ducked into an alley and banged on a door. Must have given the secret number of raps by accident, for one of your men let me in. But he took good care to keep me covered until he recognized me as the supposed assassin. Then he brought me here. That's all."

Terro waved a lordly hand to the guard. "Take him away and throw him in a cell until we get a line on his story."

BUT Cathcart interposed. "Just a moment, your 'Excellency.' May I have a word in private with you first?"

"Frisk him first," Terro commanded. The guard found nothing. "All right, guard, leave us. Well, Cathcart, what's on your mind?"

"Plenty, 'Sir.' Do you realize that a man who has proved himself clever enough to locate your hideout—"

"Then your whole long story about how you got in here isn't on the level?" Terro snapped, glowering at him.

"It's perfectly on the level. But I had already traced you to Town 13, and had figured out that you must be in a cave in the barrier wall. So I'd have found you sooner or later. But, as I was saying, don't you realize that a man as clever as that would have been able to figure out Malcolm Frain long ago. Do you realize what and where this so-called 'colony' is?"

"Now don't spring any fourth dimension stuff on me, pal. It's just a hole in the ground, which takes about twenty minutes to reach by elevator from the Frain warehouse."

"It's no such thing!" If Cathcart could but get this hulking opportunist to realize the truth, he might succeed in scaring him into negotiating with the authorities. "That 'elevator' really is a status-changing machine—it has shrunk us all to a height of less than a tenth of an inch. This forty-mile-square colony is merely a two-hundred-foot room in the Frain warehouse. I was a scientist in the outside world, Terro, before I got down-and-out and took a truck-driving job with Frain. You yourself know that they assigned me to the laboratories of the great Herr Doktor Freundlich here. Since my arrival in this colony I have spent all my spare time with scientific tests to discover the nature of this hidden world; and, believe me, We've discovered it…"

"What garbage is this," sneered Terro, but there was masked fear in his narrow-set eyes. He rang for the guard.

"Take him away and lock him up."

As Cathcart was led out through the room of the printing press, his eyes caught the wording of the flyer that was being run off. He snatched up a copy, and read it:

COMRADES ATTENTION!
BOSS FRAIN IS DEAD!
His sole heir is his daughter, Inspector Donna Frain. She had joined our cause. She is not the heartless capitalist that her father was. And she has consented to marry your Leader. By the time that this reaches you, the wedding will have been performed.
This is my last warning. Pass the word along to all those who still support the old regime, that the old regime has crumbled, and that Donna Frain herself will deal harshly with those who do not immediately join the Populist movement.
She and I jointly promise liberty and justice for all, and a free return to the Earth for those who wish it.
PUTORIUS TERRO.

Cathcart's hands clenched. His Donna married to that brute! Did she love Terro? How could she possibly love him? Cathcart writhed with an agony of jealousy. And yet was not the outcome of all this the exact result for which he himself was aiming, namely the evacuation of this tiny world before someone slipped at the control levers and snuffed them all out?

He paused irresolute, his personal feelings warring with his duty. The guard gave him a shove.

And then suddenly Cathcart's keen mind saw the flaw in the whole set-up. Donna undoubtedly knew the secret of this hidden universe, and evidently had not told Terro. Hence she was an unwilling bride. Putorius Terro would prove a worse tyrant than even Malcolm Frain; and would

stop at nothing, even the death of the flaming Donna¬—
after marrying her and thus making himself her heir. He
would drive a harsher bargain with the United States
Government than even Frain had been prepared to do. It
must be stopped.

With a wrench, Cathcart pulled away from the guard
and dashed back into the office-room.

"By God, you shan't do this!" he shouted, making a leap
across the desk at the startled Terro.

The roar of a pistol shot sounded behind him, then a
dull thump on the back of his head and he crumpled
senseless before he reached his intended victim.

CHAPTER EIGHT
Abject Terror

CATHCART found himself lying in darkness on a hard rough rocky floor. Through the cracks in the board walls, which surrounded him, he could see dim light.

He sat up unsteadily. His head ached terrifically. He raised his hand to it, and found that a wet sticky bandage was wrapped around it.

He staggered to his feet, and groped along the walls of his prison. Found a door, and rattled it. A man came, and opened a peek-hole, and peered in.

"Hello," said Cathcart.

The guard grunted.

"How long have I been out?"

"About two hours."

"When does the Leader get married?"

"None of your business."

Cathcart grinned to himself. So the wedding had not yet taken place?

"Don't you think that this is a rather scurvy treatment to give to the man who killed Boss Frain?"

"I ain't saying nothing."

"But you're willing to listen, if I give you some information that may be of value to you? It's absolutely vital to the Populist cause, but I couldn't get our Leader, Terro, to listen to it."

"So…"

"You look like a decent sort of a guy. Get me a glass of

water, and I'll give you an earful."

"I'll get you your water, but I ain't saying nothing. Don't even know if I wanna hear what you've got to say either."

The peek-hole closed. Presently it opened again and a glass of water was handed through. Cathcart drained it. He felt immeasurably better and stronger. Now to sow panic amid the forces of the enemy.

"Listen closely, and don't breathe a word to a soul." With this introduction, Cathcart plunged into an account of his scientific theories as to the nature of the hidden universe.

But the guard interrupted him with a snort. "Looney! Crazy as a bat. No wonder Terro wouldn't listen to you." He slammed shut the opening.

As Cathcart slumped disconsolately to the ground again, he tried to make himself believe that the seed of fear, which he had planted in the brain of this dull-witted fellow, might sprout and spread before it was too late.

A couple of hours later the peek-hole opened again.

"Hello…" said a familiar voice.

"Mickey!" Cathcart exclaimed.

"Shhh! Careful… I'm on guard here now for one shift. Mustn't fraternize with the prisoners you know."

"Listen, Foley. I rather figure that our great 'Leader' won't permit me to live very long, and so I'm going to make good my promise to give you the low-down on the death of Malcolm Frain—for your tabloid, when you get out of here. It ought to be quite a scoop."

"That's decent of you. Shoot."

"Remember your tipping me off once to the fact that this is a flat world? No curvature?"

"Yeah. But what has that to do with your killing Frain?

Me, I wouldn't murder a man just because the Earth is flat. But then you Harvard fellows are peculiar."

"Mickey, this is no laughing matter. Listen. I'll give you the scientific scoop of the age, and in as popular language as I'm capable of. Then it'll be up to you to play the Garrett P. Serviss with it for the press."

"Go ahead…"

THIS time, with a more sympathetic and intelligent listener, Cathcart got the science aspect of his story across. And all the news value of the story so completely transcended all other considerations in the reporter's mind, that he seemed not to be frightened at it.

"Well…ain't we got fun," Foley exclaimed when Cathcart finished. "I can just see the front-page lead: 'FRAIN'S SECRET WORLD EXPOSED. The Man Who Would be God!' Talk about your Millionaire Man of Mystery. Looks like the mystery is solved—"

"Yes, but Mickey," Cathcart soberly reminded him, "how are you going to get your story to your paper?"

"The revolution is about to triumph, and then we'll all be free," the reporter airily replied.

"I wonder. What if someone was to turn off the current in the meantime? There's no one running things, you know, with Frain dead and his daughter vanished. Most of us are just uneducated fruit-flies; we'd never be missed."

Foley paused, then said, "I hadn't thought of that."

"Well how would you handle that story if you wanted to get it across to a lot of uneducated types, instead of to the high brow readers of the New York Daily Tabloid?"

"How—would—? I getcha. I'd cut the part about the size-change. That's too goofy. I'd cover merely the fact that our light and air is fed into here artificially, and that if a power line happened to break, or if the man at the controls happened to fall asleep or quit his job—blooie! And with Frain dead, that's a lot more likely to happen, unless his daughter takes charge pronto. She's probably the only person who understands the ropes, outside of him."

"Good boy, Foley," Cathcart said approvingly. He felt somewhat assured that his reporter friend would be sure to take care of Donna.

"But look here, pal. How come, knowing all this, you killed the Boss?"

"I didn't." Cathcart then related what had actually taken place in the garden, including Malcolm Frain's tacit admission, just before the firing of the fatal shot, that Cathcart's theories of the nature of this hidden universe were correct.

"But then why does Terro give you the credit?"

"The blame, you mean. I figure he wants to queer me with Donna."

"Ahh..." Foley whistled. "So that's what he's up to. Well, I don't know. Perhaps the quickest way to get us out of here would be to let the marriage go through."

Then Cathcart played his trump card. He recounted his conversation of the giants—Frain and the Secretary of War—which his phonograph had recorded.

"The dirty, treasonous louse," Foley muttered. "So Boss Frain cared more for his lust of power than for saving his country. He deserved to get shot. And what a story this war will make." There was suddenly a noise from behind. "Damn, I've got to get out! Change of guard coming."

He slammed the cover of the peek hole shut.

Cathcart sat down again on the hard floor, well content

to believe that he had at last succeeded in planting a virus of fear that would serve for the eventual undoing of Putorius Terro, and the rescuing of Donna Frain.

And then he realized that he had omitted to ask Mickey Foley when the wedding had been set for. Nor would the new guard tell him.

But the succeeding guard, although he too would not tell Cathcart anything about the wedding or other plans of Leader Terro, did ask Cathcart with much trepidation about the danger of a cut-off of light and air from the colony; and Cathcart, taking care now to keep away from the question of size, gave the man plenty more fearsome details to increase his worry. And added the suggestion that a failure to shut off the regular night rain would drown them all like rats in a trap. Truly Mickey Foley's news-story was spreading...

The next two guards that followed seemed even more agitated, and more eager to interview Cathcart about the dangers that might lay ahead for the colony. But neither divulged anything about the wedding. Was it too late to save Donna Frain from the impending, unwelcome union?

Finally word came that the Leader, Terro, wanted to see him, and he was taken—¬this time strongly shackled—out of his cell, down the cavern, and into Headquarters once more, into the presence of Putorius Terro.

This time the swarthy man was taking no chances— behind his chair stood three determined-looking men, revolvers held alertly ready.

THE Populist Leader's tufted eyebrows contracted in a frown above his narrow-set beady eyes. "Cathcart," he said, "you aren't going to bother me much longer. But first

I thought you'd like to see the wedding. It's going to be pulled off at once."

"Does Miss Frain really want to marry you?" Cathcart blurted out.

Terro opened his slit mouth, disclosing two rows of bad teeth, and laughed. "She didn't, at first," he admitted, still laughing.

"What do you mean?"

"That is, not until I told her what my wedding present to her was going to be." Terror chuckled softly. "When she heard that she—figuratively speaking—flung her arms around my neck."

Cathcart grimaced at the thought.

Terro continued, "I'm going to give her the death of the man who killed her father. In fact, she's going to drop you herself at the wedding…" He smiled and chuckled again. "It'll be quite a moment, I assure you."

Then the guards dragged Cathcart out again, to the accompaniment of Terro's mocking laughter.

This time Cathcart was led to a part of the cavern that opened out into a huge vaulted hall. At one side jutted a ledge of rock that formed a natural stage. At the very edge of this stage stood a rough-looking wooden altar, and at one side of the stage a four-by-four beam some ten feet high was planted upright in a crack in the rocky floor. It was to this beam that Cathcart was firmly bound with ropes, a dirty disheveled figure with two days' growth of beard. One man hit him roughly on the face.

The wooden benches of the amphitheater were beginning to fill with people, who stared curiously up at him, and whispered. Had Foley's propaganda spread sufficiently, he wondered, so that he could hope to sway this audience with an appeal to save Donna Frain and themselves?

As if in answer to his speculations, one of the guards came and stuffed a handkerchief into his mouth, then tied another across his jaws to hold the first in place. Terro was taking no chances of a farewell address by his victim.

A trumpet blared, and the whole audience arose as Terro, clad in his Field Marshal uniform, entered from one side with someone who appeared to be some kind of priest or minister.

Then a military band struck up the wedding march, and Donna Frain, clad in white, and leaning on the arm of an elderly man whom Cathcart did not know, came down the aisle, followed by six of the women. Her face was set and colorless.

Cathcart tried appealingly to catch her eye. She flashed him one contemptuous glance, held her head a trifle higher, turned toward Terro and smiled. Terro smiled back possessively, and then grinned up at Cathcart.

The procession halted and the music stopped. The priest signaled to the bridegroom to step forward and claim the bride. But instead, Terro held up his hand and leaped to the platform.

"My friends," he nearly shouted. "The Boss, Malcolm Frain is dead." The crowd let out a cheer, and Donna shuddered. Terro continued, "But now we are going to make peace with the Frains, with our colony coming out on top. All of you who've been loyal to me are going to have good jobs in the Frain Industries. And part of the price of this peace is that my beautiful lady here…" He bowed toward Donna. "…is going to polish off the man who killed her father." He then reached into his waist holster and removed a revolver. "Here, dear, take this."

HE handed the automatic down, butt foremost, to Donna Frain. Cathcart strained at his bonds, and strove to spit the gag out of his mouth.

An angry murmur arose from the crowd. Someone called out, "No...he killed our enemy. He's one of us."

"Silence!" Terro shouted.

"He did not kill Boss Frain," called out a cracked voice from the back of the room.

The crowd fell into a hush and turned about.

"I did..."

All eyes leveled on a tall gaunt longhaired man who had stood up. "Leader Terro," he cried. "You shan't take the credit away from me. You assigned me the task of wiping out our oppressor. I carried out that order, and now you give this credit to another? Down with all Frains, I say." He snatched out a revolver and leveled it at Donna.

There was the sudden roar of a shot! But it was from the platform, not from the tall man in the crowd. On the edge of the platform stood Mickey Foley, smoking gun in hand. The tall man crumpled.

"Is this true, Sergeant?" Donna called up to Field Marshal Terro, and there was a sting in the word "Sergeant." She swung her own gun around toward Terro, but a nearby guard snatched it from her hand.

"You bet your boots it's true!" shouted Mickey Foley, digging his gun into Terro's ribs. "Cathcart is innocent. Tell 'em it's true, 'Sergeant!'"

"Of course, it's not true," Terro suavely replied. "The man who was just shot was—obviously—quite insane. Cathcart claims to have killed the Boss. If Cathcart is lying, then he must be not only a traitor, but a spy, too."

Cathcart tried to shout to Mickey to shoot and shoot quick. Terro was playing for time. One man alone could not hope to hold this crowd at bay for long. But not a sound came through Cathcart's gag. He strained at his ropes, and thought he felt the pole to which he was tied tilt a little.

A momentary, breathless pause ensued over the crowd, but it was broken by a man rushing into the hall, frantically shouting, "It's happened! The light and air have been shut off! And it's beginning to rain—hard, very hard! Sooner or later we're all going to drown…"

Terro took advantage of the confusion to wheel about and wrestle the gun out of Foley's hand. "That's a complete lie!" he shouted.

Cathcart then gave a big heave, and the foot of the stake lifted—just barely—out of the crack in the rocky floor. He leaned far forward, and crashed to the ground, striking Terro squarely with the top of the pole, and felling him.

The whole auditorium was in an uproar. Foley rushed over to Cathcart, cut his bounds, and yanked off his gag. Then picked up his fallen weapon…

He then pumped several shots into the sprawled body of Putorius Terro!

"Let's get out of here, pal," he shouted.

"If the end of this world has come, what's the use?" Cathcart asked, staring around for Donna, who had been swallowed up in the crowd.

"Nuts!" Foley snapped. "I planted that guy in the crowd."

"Then we have to save Donna…"

"Nuts again! There's only one way out of this cave— the dirt tunnel. I know a short cut to reach it. Donna'll be in the crowd all right. The thing to do is to get to the tunnel ahead of the mob, and preserve order. Come on!"

CATHCART grabbed a gun out of the hand of a bewildered guard and followed Foley into a narrow slit in the wall, through which they groped for quite a ways in the darkness, finally emerging into the main cavern again and into a seething crowd surging toward the exit.

The exit was hopelessly jammed. No one would ever get out unless order could be restored.

Into the jam of people waded Cathcart and Foley, clubbing right and left with their pistol butts. They reached the tunnel mouth but were swept aside by the milling throng. They shouted, but could not make themselves heard. Then Cathcart fired his weapon at the ceiling. Splinters of rock fell, and the echoing sound of the shot reverberated through the cavern. The noise halted the crowd momentarily and they surged back in unison away from the sound of this new menace.

"Listen to me," Cathcart commanded. "We're armed, and we'll shoot to kill!"

The crowd began to quiet down. But scanning their heads, Cathcart saw a gun leveled at him. He promptly fired and dropped the fellow, who grabbed at his shoulder.

"Now will you listen?" he bellowed. "Fall back there, all of you, or I'll shoot again. Anyone with common sense and a cool head please come forward and help." Several men elbowed their way out and took their places beside him. Cathcart spoke quickly to them. "Good. Now you force the crowd back, and line them up in single file."

Speedily, the line was formed. Foley, at the tunnel mouth, let them through one at a time.

"Has anyone seen Donna Frain?" Cathcart shouted.

A shout came from the crowd, "She's over here."

Cathcart waved his arm. "Let her come forward."

An angry grumble arose. One surly-looking man called

out, "Why should she get out ahead of us?"

"Because the sooner she reaches the controls," Cathcart answered, "the sooner we'll all be safe. She's the only person who knows how to stop the rain and turn the light and air on again."

A moment later Donna Frain, in a much torn and bedraggled wedding gown, was passed forward.

She raised eyes full of gratitude to her rescuer. "Forgive me for having doubted you," she begged. "I've been a beast."

Cathcart's heart went out to her. But he had responsibilities to the people. "Donna," he said sadly, "I hate to have to suspect you. But before I let you out of here, you've got to make me a promise."

"Such impudence…" She whispered.

"No promise, no get out."

"Well…what is it?"

"That your troops will not interfere with my evacuating this cave, once you are on the outside and in command again."

She nodded.

"On your word of honor."

"On my word of honor."

"Okay, Foley, let her through. Goodbye, Donna, I'll be seeing you." And he turned his attention back toward supervising the line; as, head held high, the girl swept by him.

FINALLY the last person in the line was through. The men who had helped Cathcart hesitated. "All right for us to go now?" one of them inquired.

"We ought to search the cave for the injured," Cathcart asserted. "A lot must have been trampled on."

"Nuts on that!" cried Mickey Foley. "Hell's probably a-popping outside; and the sooner we get out, the better. If the Town 13 hospital is still in operation, we can send some stretcher-bearers in here after the wounded. If not, then the wounded might as well die in here as outside, I read in a medical column once that no one but a doctor ought ever try to move an injured person."

They all then crawled out of the cavern, and out of the house in which the tunnel ended—looks of surprise coming across all their faces.

It was day outside, broad daylight.

Neither the air-supply nor the bright, diffused light above the clouds had been turned off, nor was it raining. They found the doctors, nurses, and interns of the local hospital sticking to their posts, though every other member of the community, both lay and official, was streaking toward the Headquarters City in a subdued panic.

Hurriedly they told the hospital staff about the injured in the cave.

Then Cathcart said, "We've got to head off this stampede somehow."

"What's the matter with leaving that to the authorities?" Foley objected. "You seem to think you're some sort of a superman all of a sudden."

Cathcart grimaced. "I made this people listen to me once, didn't I?"

Foley nodded, a smile on his face. "Yeah…you did."

"I can make them do it again."

"But how will you get ahead of them? Every auto in town has probably been taken or stolen."

"I've a car that they won't have taken, down the road a little ways. Come on."

The two of them set off at a quick jog out of town.

Cathcart found the car still standing where he had left it. It was a simple matter to replace the distributor-head.

Then he drove away from the main highway and took a less direct route that wasn't choked with refugees. And he forced the car to its utmost speed.

"I ought to get to a telegraph station and send in an account of all this," Foley commented. Then he started laughing out loud. "Oh, boy…what a story…"

It was the only remark by either of them as they roared along.

When they reached Headquarters City, Cathcart slowed down and glanced at his wristwatch. "Five forty¬-five," he announced. "Nightfall in fifteen minutes. And then what?"

THERE were no guards at the usual posts on the outskirts. All the streets were deserted, except for refugees straggling in. Abandoned automobiles blocked the streets. Leaving their car, Cathcart and Foley got out and made their way on foot toward the Administration Building. It too was empty.

They turned toward the building that housed the "status-changing machine" against the face of the barrier wall. Cathcart glanced at his watch again. Six fifteen, but still daylight!

"Someone is asleep at the switchboard," was his tight-lipped comment.

Foley chuckled. "I've got a better explanation than that. Miss Frain has phoned them to leave the lights on. That's one advantage of a 'controlled economy.' "

Finally Cathcart and Foley edged their way to an open space. In spite of pushing from behind, the front lines of the crowd were holding back in evident trepidation of something ahead.

Ringed about the face of the building was a semi-circle of soldiers, armed with machine guns, rifles, and hand grenades. And behind them on the steps of a doorway stood Donna Frain (in trim black uniform again), Professor Freundlich, and a small group of grim looking Inspectors.

"We're not afraid of their guns!" shouted someone in the mob. "Come on! We'll die here anyway if they turn off the light and the air."

CHAPTER NINE
The Death Ray

THE crowd began to edge slowly forward.

Donna Frain took a microphone in her slim hand, and her clear calm voice sounded over a loud-speaker high up on the face of the building: "Colonists! Look what time it is. Nearly half past six, and daylight is still with us. Is not this evidence enough of my good faith?" Donna paused, then continued, "You are all perfectly safe; but this one small status-changing machine is the only exit from this world. If you try to rush it, many will be killed by my guards. And, even if you finally overpower my guards and reach the machine, you certainly won't know how to operate it—you might even wreck it, and then none of us will ever get out of here alive."

"Let us out!" a frantic voice shouted from somewhere in the crowd. The cry was taken up and echoed forth, drowning out Donna's words.

Cathcart jumped in front of the crowd and held up his hand. The hubbub quieted somewhat.

"How many of you are Populists?" he shouted. "Don't be afraid to speak up!" He paused and pointed toward himself. "I'd like to be your new leader—at least for the time being. I got you out of the cave, didn't I? Well, I'll get you out of here, too. All who were in the cave, hold up your hands." A few hands shot up. "Come on! All of you..." More hands raised upward.

Then toward Donna's group on the steps, Cathcart said,

"And I got you out of the cave too, young lady; don't forget that."

An angry rumble arose in the crowd, interspersed with some laughter.

"Let's get those hands up again!" Cathcart shouted. This time quite a number showed. "You who are holding up your hands—you at least are Populists. Why aren't we all Populists? For it's only by sticking together that we can win our freedom."

"Shall I shoot him down?" asked one of Donna's machine-gunners grimly.

Donna looked at the guard incredulously and hurriedly shook her head. "Have you lost your senses? Let him speak, I'll deal with him myself later."

"Everyone hold up your hands!" Cathcart commanded. The crowd obeyed, almost to a man. "There…now we are all Populists. Are you with me?"

Many in the crowd voiced their approval.

Mickey Foley snorted contemptuously, though. "Come on, Cathcart, this sounds like a bunch of over-the-top hokum. Now let's give three rousing cheers for the old Alma Mater."

Ignoring Foley's cynicism, Cathcart turned back toward Donna and her group. "What do you have to say to that, young lady?"

There was scattered cheers from the crowd.

"Merely this," she said, her clear voice coming out of the loudspeaker. "As I was about to inform you when I was interrupted, these guns are not my only defense. Your new leader here has doubtless told you what a great scientist he is." There was a certain amount of scorn in her voice. "Well, a greater scientist, his teacher, stands here beside me." She nodded toward Freundlich. "Between me…" She pointed to herself and her guards. "…and you…" Her arms flourished toward the crowd. "…is an impenetrable wall of energy, set up by Herr Doktor Freundlich. I don't want to see anybody hurt, but if any of you should attempt to rush our position, my machine guns do not need to fire upon you, for this wall of energy would destroy you in a puff of smoke as fast as you reached it. We have important work to be done here, so now I want you all to return peacefully to your homes, or shall you be foolhardy enough to tinker with a device that is essentially a death ray?"

Most of the crowd swayed backward.

"Do you think that's really some kind of a death ray?" Foley whispered.

Cathcart considered. "I—I doubt it," he declared. "Freundlich had nothing like that in his laboratories when I was with him. It's ridiculous to think that there's been time enough for him to build a device like this since Donna escaped and reached here."

The crowd began to rumble ominously.

"Donna…you little fool," Cathcart muttered to himself, then he leaned toward Foley and whispered softly, "I had them eating out of my hand a minute ago, and now she's spoiled it." He then stepped up and spoke loudly to the crowd. "With all due respect Miss Frain, I think your death ray is a fake. I've worked closely with Dr. Freundlich almost every day since I've been here." He gave a slight bow in the doctor's direction. "And I know every item in his laboratories. He has no such machine to my knowledge."

"No?" came Donna's cool voice out of the loudspeaker. "Observe…"

THE door of the building opened and two soldiers emerged, dragging between them what appeared to be a body-bag of some sort containing what appeared to be a human body. They dragged this down the steps and through the cordon of machine guns. There they halted. The crowd watched, fascinated. Then the soldiers heaved the body-bag toward the crowd.

It vanished in a puff of smoke!

A long-drawn gasp escaped the crowd.

"The she-devil!" Cathcart exclaimed under his breath. Then aloud he shouted, "All right, all right! Let's not panic."

A few of the people fled, but most remained, jeering Donna Frain and her companions.

"Please... Please!" Cathcart implored the nervous onlookers. "Let's all try to stay together. Isn't this demonstration an added reason for us all to be unified? Against such weapons only our unity can prevail. I'll pit my own knowledge of science against that of Doctor Freundlich. Are you with me?"

A hesitant cry of approval boomed from the fickle crowd, encouraged by Mickey Foley.

Turning proudly back toward the group on the steps, Cathcart said, "Donna, will you please let me through your energy shield so we can discuss terms of peace?"

She hesitated for a few moments, then nodded reluctantly. Doctor Freundlich then opened a switch beside him.

"Want me along?" asked Foley.

Cathcart shook his head. "You stay here and carry on. Try to keep the crowd calm." He looked glaringly at Donna. "Heaven knows she hasn't." Then he turned to the crowd and said, "I'm leaving Mr. Foley here in charge until I return. Please do as he says." Cathcart stepped forward.

Ignoring Donna, he turned to his former patron. "Dr. Freundlich," he asked tensely, "how did you devise this force-barrier and set it up so quickly?"

The little man beamed, then whispered, "My young friend, it was as you would say, all a bluff. There is no force-shield."

"But that body-bag...we saw it destroyed."

"A mere dummy, filled with silver¬-flash powder. But it served to hold the mob in check."

"Are you crazy?" Cathcart replied in a low voice. "It could have started a riot and gotten us all killed..."

"Dr. Freundlich," Donna weakly snapped, "you talk too much..."

Cathcart turned toward her with surprise, then pity. "You poor kid," he said, shaking his head. "You're beaten and battered, tired and depressed. And I've been thinking of you as a heartless murderess." He sighed in relief. "I'm glad your 'death ray' was just a hoax."

She swayed from fatigue. Cathcart caught her.

"Careful, son," cautioned Freundlich. "The crowd is watching."

"Damn the crowd!" Cathcart exclaimed, drawing her closer.

"Oh, Bob, I'm so tired," the girl sighed, nestling against him. "I was trying to carry on as Dad would have done, but I guess it is too much for me. Inspector Cathcart," she said, looking into his eyes, "please take over."

"Hey, what's the big idea?" yelled someone in the impatient crowd.

Cathcart seized the microphone and held it right up to Donna's mouth. "Repeat after me. I, Donna—"

She looked impishly up at him, and covered the mike with her hand, "—do take you, Robert?"

"Hell, no!"

Her face flushed red.

"I mean not just now," Cathcart whispered in her ear. "We've got to get settle with these folks right now. Here's what you need to say: 'I, Donna Frain, pledge my word of honor to get all you people out of this colony just as fast as is feasible.' "

SHE repeated the words to the anxious crowd and continued, "Meanwhile I guarantee to maintain light and air. You have my promise. And to show my good faith I agree to live among you as a hostage until all this is accomplished…"

Someone in the front of the crowd called out in a soft voice, "Guess we can't ask for much more than that."

"Well let's have a big hand for Robert Cathcart and Donna Frain!" shouted Mickey Foley, almost sarcastically.

Some cheers and light applause poured forth.

Cathcart took the microphone. "And now," he said, "in order for all of us to show the good faith of Populists, let's return to our homes. Those of us who live too far to travel back tonight will be lodged here—in the barracks, or quartered in homes in the area. Those of you who live in nearby towns will be taken by bus and official cars." Turning to one of the officers beside him, he commanded, "Go ahead and march the machine gun unit back to their barracks."

"Is it safe, Miss?" the officer objected, doubtfully staring at her.

"Everything's fine. Please obey him," Donna listlessly replied.

Cathcart continued, "The 'death-ray' is lifted, and the troops are dispersing. Report over to the Administration Building for quarters or transportation. I want volunteers to run the cars." Cathcart singled out three of the men. "Here you, Inspector Jenks, take charge of assignment to quarters. You pick out chauffeurs, Inspector Hansen. Inspector Petzold, take charge of transportation."

The crowd began to break up.

"Just a minute," Cathcart shouted. He glanced at his wristwatch. "It is now seven-thirty. The sun will set at eight tonight by special dispensation."

A hearty laugh went up from the crowd. Cathcart turned to Donna Frain. "Please get the control-room at once by deferred telephone, and order them to shut off the ultra-violet lights at promptly 8:00 p.m., our time."

"You know about the lights, and how we telephone back to Earth?"

"I know a lot of things, young lady."

"I wonder," she mused.

TAKING Donna by the arm, Cathcart led her down the steps and toward the Administration Building. Foley joined them.

Donna Frain stiffened and shuddered. Then relaxed and smiled sadly toward Foley. "My poor dear father is dead," she said, "and so someone must bear the title of 'Boss' until we clean up this mess, which his delusions of grandeur created. So why not let Bob here be the new 'Boss'?"

"I really think the title should pass by heredity to the next of kin," Cathcart objected, as they entered Donna's office.

"And then by marriage to her husband," Donna added

in a low voice.

He smiled and glanced at Foley. "Why...I believe some woman is proposing to me." Then hurriedly he said, "And I accept before she withdraws the offer." He slipped one arm around her waist and drew her close.

Dr. Freundlich came in, too. Donna then put through a deferred call, instructing that the nightfall period commence at eight o'clock.

Then Freundlich, his pale blue eyes beaming on Donna and Cathcart and Foley, asked, "And what of the threatened European invasion?"

"You knew of that too?" Donna said, a slight look of surprise on her face.

The three men nodded.

"I tried to dissuade Father," she said, "but he insisted on his...his price. I am now prepared to repeat his offer to save America, but I shall insist upon another and quite different price."

Cathcart stared at her with surprise. "What do you mean? Why, I thought—"

"You thought I was more patriotic than my father—and you were right. My father used his great scientific powers selfishly; I intend to use them for the welfare of humanity. So my ultimatum is that America cede to Frain Industries all the wastelands in North Dakota and Montana, in exchange for this colony. We'll move our colonists there, and start afresh. What Father could do with the barren floor of a warehouse, I, with you three men to help me, ought to be able to accomplish with a mere wasteland."

"What a story," Mickey Foley exclaimed.

"What a girl," cried Cathcart, gathering her to him.

THE END